FOUR PEAKS

The Final Campaign

Craig Main

Other Books by the Author:

Shadow of the Mogollon Rim
Raiders of Salt River Canyon

authorHOUSE®

AuthorHouse™
1663 Liberty Drive
Bloomington, IN 47403
www.authorhouse.com
Phone: 1-800-839-8640

First published by AuthorHouse 1/25/2011

ISBN: 978-1-4520-8136-6 (sc)
ISBN: 978-1-4520-8137-3 (e)

Library of Congress Control Number: 2010914968

Printed in the United States of America

This book is printed on acid-free paper.

All photos and drawings by the author

All Scripture quotations are taken or adapted from the King James Version of the Bible.

Characters in this novel sometimes speak words that are adapted from the King James Version of the Bible.

This novel is dedicated to
Those who serve at every level of law enforcement:
Federal
State
Commonwealth
County
Parish
City
Town

Thank you
For your diligent service.

A heartfelt
Thank You
To my friends
And
Tireless editors of this novel,

Raymond & Margaret McGirt

A very special
Thank You
To

Director, Carol Thornton-Anderson,

And her staff at

Melton Public Library

And to

Friends of the Library

For

All their support over the past several years.

¡Gracias!

CAST OF CHARACTERS

Clint Wells, a former Texas Ranger, was a hardworking Arizona rancher devoted to the breeding of top-quality riding horses. But he was also a long-standing reserve member of the Arizona Rangers. The campaign he was about to embark upon was one of the toughest he had ever faced. Even bigger than the raid on the outlaws at the Mogollon Rim Ranch or the assault on the raiders of Salt River Canyon.

Captain Jim O'Bryan, the new leader of a small group of Arizona Rangers stationed at Fort Verde, was given the biggest assignment of his career. He was to lead his rangers on a mission to Four Peaks in the southern range of the Mazatzal Mountains. The largest known contingent of Arizona-based outlaws was operating from a base camp in Wild Burro Canyon. The odds were not in favor of the rangers—and some would not survive.

Butch Kantrell, outlaw leader *extraordinaire*, was known far and wide as one of the toughest outlaws in the southwest. His gang of nearly fifty cutthroats had done it all: arson, robbery, extortion, murder and rape. With the capable backing of his two brutal cohorts—Russ Thorpe and a renegade Apache by the name of Two Scars—there seemed to be no way to stop their violent trek across the Arizona Territory.

Henry Watts, special envoy to the governor of the Arizona Territory, was widely known to be a man of unquestionable integrity. His assignment: Assemble a large group of lawmen from all agencies and clean out the nest of outlaws hiding in a secluded canyon in the shadow of Four Peaks.

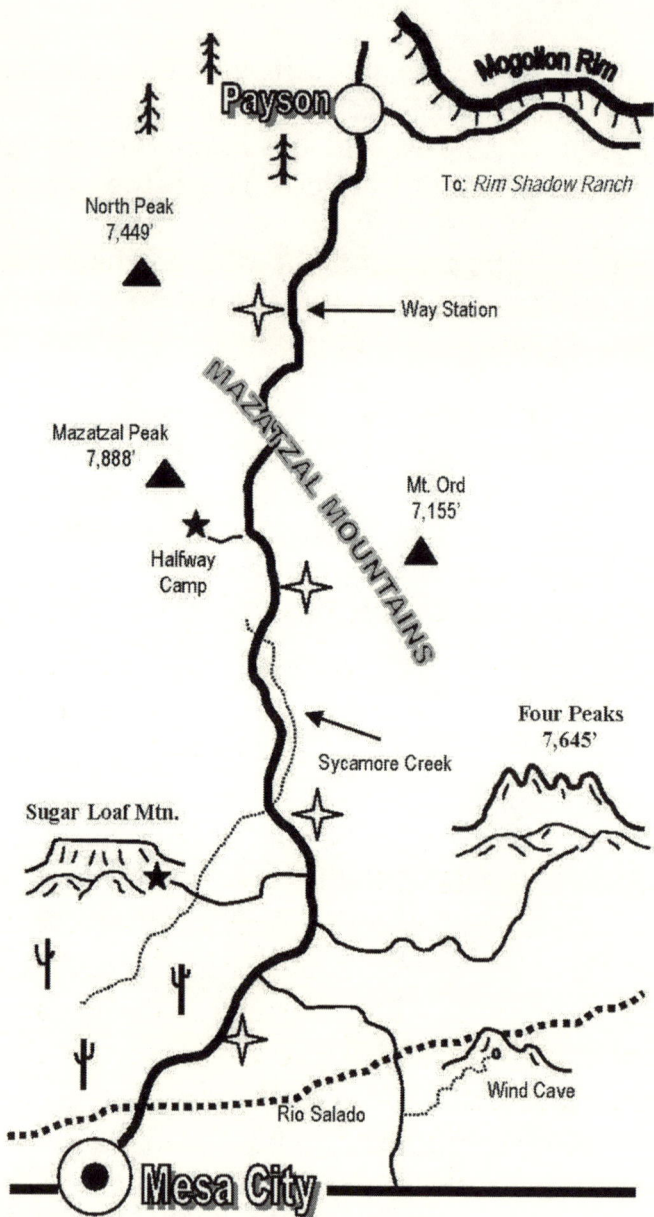

FOUR PEAKS: The Final Campaign

Payson

Mogollon Rim

To: *Rim Shadow Ranch*

North Peak
7,449'

Way Station

MAZATZAL MOUNTAINS

Mazatzal Peak
7,888'

Mt. Ord
7,155'

Halfway
Camp

Four Peaks
7,645'

Sycamore Creek

Sugar Loaf Mtn.

Wind Cave

Rio Salado

Mesa City

Chapter One

Tuesday, October 6th.

Clint Wells was resting comfortably in a padded rocking chair on the front porch of his ranch house. He had a steaming cup of black coffee in one hand, and an unopened letter in the other. The letter was embossed with a Flagstaff postmark. He was somewhat hesitant to open it.

Not twenty minutes ago, Clint had been hard at work at the nearby Double Creek Ranch assisting his best friend and business partner, Robert Lynne, with the speedy turnaround of the stagecoach. The job involved swapping out the four-horse team, unloading supplies, and gathering the mail destined for nearby ranches. On this rather pleasant fall day, Clint was on the receiving end of one of those letters.

The stage line makes its run every day, except Sunday, between Show Low and Payson. On Monday, Wednesday and Friday it travels west; on Tuesday, Thursday and Saturday it travels east. Since there is only one stagecoach arrival per business day, Clint does not have to spend more than two hours on each occurrence away from his own ranching business—the breeding, training, and selling of top-quality riding horses.

The Double Creek Ranch is primarily a cattle ranch, but four years ago—to increase operating income—it became a way station, as well, for the Tonto Basin Stage Line.

Robert's ranch borders Clint's ranch on the east. Together, both ranches incorporate a vast area between Christopher Creek and Tonto Creek. A wonderful, thick forest of ponderosa pine covers most of the land between the creeks. Several large, lush, green meadows are scattered throughout the properties. A small herd of elk is often seen grazing in one of these meadows.

The 120 acres that make up Clint's Rim Shadow Ranch were purchased from Robert more than four years ago. While there have been several opportunities since then to purchase additional land, Clint has refrained from doing so. He is more than satisfied with the acreage that he currently owns.

Every foal born at Clint's ranch is descended from his big Thoroughbred stallion, Liberty. In the past four years, Liberty has sired over twenty-five colts from Clint's modest stable of twenty high-quality brooding mares.

Furthermore, breeding is not limited to Clint's personal stock of dams; Liberty also fetches a high-dollar fee for stud services sought by ranch owners throughout the territory. In fact, Robert Lynne had his blue-ribbon Quarter Horse, Star, bred by Clint's stallion last year. In late April, Star gave birth to a fine little filly. Robert's wife, Rebecca, named her Lilly.

Shortly after Clint opened his ranch for business (in the fall of 1892), he married Springerville resident, Lisa

Reavis. They had one child together—a girl they named Lena. Lena is now three years old, and growing like a weed. Clint is thankful that his daughter inherited her mother's joyful spirit—along with her bright green eyes and auburn red hair. Lena is, without question, the "apple" of Clint's eye.

Clint is no longer married to Lisa. Cal Amare, an outlaw on the lam, killed her in the fall of 1894. Some said it was an accidental shooting, while others claimed it was on purpose. In either case, Lisa is still gone—buried atop a small knoll about fifty yards west of the ranch house.

Robert's sister, Connie, is Clint's new wife. She tirelessly supported Clint throughout his long period of grieving. She even assisted with the operation of his ranch following Lisa's death—spending countless hours working alongside Clint from sunup to sundown. Connie has always been a very loving and caring wife *and* stepmother. Lena bonded quickly to Connie after the untimely death of her mother.

Clint, at this moment in time, wasn't thinking about Lisa, Lena, Connie, or his ranch. He was staring at the letter in his hand. It was from his friend and fellow ranger, Tom Williamson.

Tom, a charter member of the Arizona Rangers, started out as a first sergeant, was later promoted to captain, and is now a major. He is currently in charge of field operations at the regional headquarters located in Flagstaff. A *desk* job, he's quick to tell you, that he's thankful to have.

In earlier times, Clint had ridden alongside his friend on a couple of key campaigns in central Arizona. The biggest campaign, without any disagreement, was the raid on Wes Baden's vast Mogollon Rim Ranch. Baden was not only one of the largest cattle ranchers in Arizona, but an unrepentant lawbreaker as well. He was guilty of providing a safe haven for many wanted fugitives, and for allowing his gang of cutthroat riders to kill anyone that wandered onto, or near, his land.

In the summer of 1892, Baden and his roguish outfit were put out of business by the valiant rangers. The defiant sixty-year-old rancher did not survive the raid, nor did his top gun hand, Billy Blackheart, a.k.a. the Tonto Basin Kid. The Kid, true to his nature, refused to be taken alive, and was ultimately killed in a hail of gunfire.

The second biggest campaign occurred in the fall of 1894. It involved the defeat of a band of raiders hiding out in a makeshift shack at the bottom of scenic Salt River Canyon. Only five of the eleven raiders initially survived the courageous assault launched by the rangers on that action-packed day. Cole Miner, an eighteen-year-old killer and thief, escaped during the assault. Cal Amare, Aikey Hart, Tull Oaks and Forrest Woods were taken into custody. Sadly, Ranger Jess McCain lost his life when Cole Miner later ambushed him. While fleeing to avoid capture, the young outlaw tried to shoot it out with his pursuers, but he couldn't match the speed and accuracy of Ranger Clint Wells.

Jess was buried atop a low ridge overlooking the beautiful rushing waters of the Salt River. Miner was buried in a shallow grave a mile south of the canyon where Clint caught up to him. Scrub growth and cacti surround his grave.

With the four remaining raiders in custody, it appeared that everything was neatly "sewed up" and moving forward as it should. But, as the rangers traveled north to Show Low with their prisoners, things started to unravel—with disastrous results.

Even though sincere efforts were made to save him, Tull Oaks died en route from shock and blood poisoning due to a nasty gunshot wound to his thigh. During the night, Oaks' pals, Amare and Hart, managed to escape on foot. And, before taking flight, Amare fatally stabbed his outlaw companion, Woods, for cooperating with the rangers. The two cagey fugitives made their way to Show Low, misappropriated some horses and guns, and then rode west toward Payson. By pure chance, they stopped at Clint's ranch looking to steal fresh horses.

As previously mentioned, Amare, determined as always to avoid capture, ended up tragically murdering Clint's wife, Lisa. The final outcome: Amare and Hart died that day at the ranch. Clint killed Amare, and another person at the scene killed Hart.

Clint had vowed on that terrible day that he would never again ride with the rangers, but over time, God healed his broken heart. Not long after that, he carefully rethought his opposition to helping the rangers fight crime in the Arizona Territory. A few months ago, after consulting with Connie, he let Williamson know that he was emotionally and mentally fit, and ready for duty. Williamson had been elated by the news, and took immediate steps that day to see to it that Clint would one day be properly rewarded for his past service to the Arizona Rangers.

Clint opened the letter and began reading.

Thursday, October 1, 1896

Dear Clint,

> *How are you? I hope all is well. Sorry I haven't been in touch for such a long, long time. I don't know where the time goes. The older I get—the faster it slips by.*
>
> *Clint, the reason for my letter is to let you know that Captain Jim O'Bryan, from the Fort Verde ranger post, will be stopping by to see you. He is seeking your invaluable help with a large-scale campaign in the lower range of the Mazatzal Mountains. To be more precise—near Four Peaks. I hope you will be free to join him on this campaign of utmost importance. Jim will provide you with all the details when he arrives at your ranch. That should be around the seventh of October.*
>
> *I know you and Jim are great friends, and that he will be warmly greeted by you.*
>
> *There is one other bit of news I should tell you about. The territorial governor has seen fit to disband the rangers. His political advisors have convinced him that there are plenty of other law enforcement agencies to do the job we've been doing these past few years. I believe it will take effect the first of the year. It rather saddens me.*
>
> *Other than that, I don't know much, unless I forgot to tell you that I finally got married after all these many years. Her name is Linda. She's very nice. You and Connie would like her a lot.*
>
> *God bless you and your family. I hope to visit you next spring.*

Your friend always,

Tom Williamson

Clint took a deep breath, and let it out slowly. He folded the letter back up and returned it to its envelope. Though he had agreed to help the rangers, he certainly didn't care for that portion of the letter requesting his help with another *large-scale* campaign. He knew his wife, Connie, would be even more upset than he was at the moment. He dreaded telling her.

Before coming to Arizona, Clint had been a ranger in Texas for many years—from the time he was twenty-one until he turned thirty-seven.

Clint never considered the possibility that he would ever again be involved with law enforcement after he departed his home in Texas for Arizona. But his reputation, it seemed, had followed him. It wasn't very long before he was being recruited by the Arizona Rangers.

Clint has been assisting the rangers as a reservist since the summer of 1892. So far, he has been a vital part of two key campaigns (those previously mentioned), and a dozen or more less significant sorties. To this day, he is exceedingly thankful to God that he survived a near-fatal gunshot wound to the head—compliments of the outlaw Frank Carver during the raid on the Mogollon Rim Ranch. A shallow scar was still visible just above his left temple.

Now forty-one, Clint was thirty-seven when he signed on with the Arizona Rangers. The revelation that the rangers would be disbanded in three months was not unhappy news to him. He was rather glad that his long career as a lawman was coming to an end. He had seen more than his share of the worst that society had to offer. It was certainly time to put away the badge forever, and concentrate exclusively on his family and his ranching business.

The only thing that troubled Clint was the fact that some of his best friends would be out of a job. He hoped that they would all find similar work with some county or municipality. His dear friend, Will Clowers, left the rangers shortly after the Salt River Canyon campaign to fill the position of sheriff in Show Low—a position left vacant by his old friend, Ken Hannagan. At age sixty-three, Hannagan thought it best to retire and enjoy what time he had left on planet earth doing something far safer. Hannagan and his wife presently operate a boarding house in Show Low.

The seventh! That's tomorrow! Clint suddenly realized, nearly shouting the words aloud.

Clint hastily rose from his comfortable rocking chair and went into the house. He placed Williamson's letter on his small wooden desk, and then scurried off to the kitchen for another cup of coffee. His mind suddenly focused on Connie. He wished that she were home so he could show her the letter and get her reaction to it behind him. But he realized that her arrival was still many hours away.

Eighteen months ago, Connie and her aunt, Helen Myers, opened a mercantile store and café at Christopher Creek. The new business venture requires Connie's presence Monday through Saturday from nine o'clock in the morning until five o'clock in the afternoon.

Seeing the store and café come to fruition brought a great deal of fulfillment to Connie and her aunt. And fortunately, the store and café turned out to be a good financial investment. The monetary return has far exceeded all their expectations.

One factor contributing to the success of the café is the fact that the stagecoach stops there six times per week to allow the passengers to eat lunch. In the past, the passengers ate a cold, brown-bagged sandwich that was prepared for them at the Double Creek Ranch way station.

Another factor for the café doing so well came about when Connie and her aunt adopted the same successful method of serving their stage passengers that the famous Fred Harvey chain of restaurants utilized to serve their rail passengers at stops along the route of the Santa Fe railway. That being: limit the menu, prepare the meals ahead of time, and have them ready to serve when the passengers arrived. This prevented long delays, allowing the railway company to maintain its all-important timetable.

Clint's thoughts were suddenly interrupted by a knock at the door. It was Chip Bowman, a young lad that Clint had hired recently to help with the ranch duties. Though only a mere twenty years old, he had a good work ethic. His sizeable knowledge of horses made him a valuable asset to Clint and his business.

Chip had drifted down to Arizona from Wyoming after the death of his parents. He initially punched cattle for the Hash Knife outfit for several months, but quickly grew tired of being in the saddle from sunrise to sunset. He had always been good with horses, and when he heard about Clint's horse ranch, he hastily came calling. Clint hired him following a two-week trial period. So far, things have worked out well for both employee and employer.

Working for Clint is a delight for Chip. He found his boss to be a godly man, as well as patient and easy-going. Furthermore, he's happy that his boss pays a decent wage. In addition to his regular pay, he's also eligible for bonus pay. And last, but certainly not least, he appreciates the free room and board. Since there's currently no ranch foreman, Clint has Chip housed in the upgraded foreman's private room at the south end of the bunkhouse.

Chip's room measures ten-by-twelve feet, and has an appearance of spaciousness. It has some nice upgrades over the open barracks-like room that adjoins his room. The foreman's room has a full-sized bed, a table with two chairs, curtains on the windows, and a nice woven rug covering most of the floor. Lastly, it has its own small woodstove. In comparison, the adjoining room has four cot-like beds, a bare pine floor, and a small table with four chairs in the middle of the room. A fireplace is located at the north end of the room.

"Come in, Chip!" Clint yelled from the kitchen.

Chip removed his hat and entered the spacious living room. "Pardon my intrusion, Mr. Wells, but I just wanted to let ya know that one of the broodin' mares got kicked by that sorry dun of mine. I don't think it's too serious, but ya might want to have a look at her just the same."

"Thanks, Chip, for let'n me know. I'll take a look at her in a minute," Clint replied, seemingly unconcerned by the news, as he placed his now empty coffee cup in the sink.

"Well, sir, I'll be git'n back to the corral."

"Chip, did you take time to eat lunch while I was over at Robert's place?"

"No, sir. I got so busy that I lost track of time."

"Well, come over here and sit down. I'll fix us both some lunch. That mare can wait a few minutes."

Clint and Chip discussed the afternoon's chores while wolfing down their sandwiches. There was still much to be done before Connie got home. For one thing, they were expecting a local rancher to stop by around three o'clock to look over several two-year-old colts that Clint had available for sale. Clint was dearly hoping to sell one of the colts before the day was over. After all, that's what paid the bills.

Selling a horse made Chip very happy as well—because he received five percent of the selling price as a bonus for caring for, and prepping the horse for the new owner.

"Guess we had best get to it," Clint said.

"Yes, sir. Reckon that buyer will be showin' up here in a couple of hours. I need to brush those colts down again. I want 'em all to look like a shiny new penny."

"Good idea. And speakin' of pennies—I hope to get a *pretty penny* for one of 'em," Clint chirped.

Clint and Chip quickly cleared the table and deposited their soiled dishes in the sink. A moment later, they were out the door and headed for the corral that contained the colts.

* * * * *

Captain Jim O'Bryan was presently en route to Clint's ranch via Payson. Accompanying him were veteran rangers Dave Martin and Geoff Tingle—and a newcomer, Titus Green. They were approximately twenty miles south of Fort Verde. The first leg of their journey would take them to Payson. After a good night's rest in a Payson hotel, they would press on to Clint's ranch—arriving tomorrow afternoon.

The campaign that Jim and his men were embarking upon would be extremely dangerous, and bigger than anything they had tackled before. A lot was at stake.

The new territorial governor had issued a mandate: *Clean out the last big stronghold of outlaws that were presently terrorizing the citizens of the Arizona Territory.*

The governor was not only calling on the rangers, but on every law enforcement agency in the territory. No town marshal or county sheriff was exempt. The governor was even asking for help from the United States marshal's office.

This gang was said to be bigger than the one that Wes Baden harbored at his Mogollon Rim Ranch, or the one that was hiding in Salt River Canyon. It was estimated that nearly fifty men rode with Butch Kantrell. Many of the gang members were wanted for crimes they had committed outside of Arizona. These men had drifted into the territory over a period of months in hopes of hiding from their pursuers.

The time had finally come to do something about their relentless robbing and killing of innocent civilians. It would certainly take a joint effort to defeat them. And that was what the governor had in mind.

"Captain, how many lawmen do ya think will show up at Four Peaks?" twenty-seven-year-old Dave Martin asked his boss as he adjusted himself in the saddle.

"Haven't a clue, Dave. Maybe fifty or sixty men—if we are fortunate. Not every town has a deputy they can send. I think most of our help will come out of Phoenix. I hear they have a rather large department of officers."

Dave had one more question lingering in his mind. "Will there be any rangers from the Tucson district showin' up at Four Peaks?" he asked.

"I doubt it. They've got a wagon load of problems of their own along the border to take care of."

"Cap', do ya think our friend, Clint Wells, will be joinin'

us?" thirty-year-old Geoff Tingle asked as he wiped at the back of his neck with a frayed and soiled bandanna that he had moistened with water from his canteen.

"It's hard to say, Geoff. He's pretty much fed up with huntin' outlaws after that tragic killin' of his wife by Cal Amare. Last I heard, Clint was still blamin' himself for Amare's escape from custody," the forty-year-old leader replied as he popped the cap on his canteen for a necessary drink.

"Yeah, that was a terrible deal," Geoff replied. "Maybe, if Dave and I had been with y'all, that *skunk* and his pal would not have gotten away. I heard how short-handed y'all were. I'm glad those two stinkin' cowards ended up as fodder for the worms."

"I'm tellin' you the truth," Jim began, "we were all bone-tired … and all the while tryin' to keep tabs on four prisoners. One of 'em was even shot up pretty bad. He died the same night that Amare and Hart escaped.

"And worst of all, that Amare feller was so despicable that he even killed one of his own men durin' his escape. Stuck that poor ol' boy in the heart with a knife that he had hidden away in his boot," Jim said as he retold a small portion of the story of the Salt River Canyon campaign. (This was done mostly for the benefit of Titus, who had no prior knowledge of the campaign and its disastrous and sad outcome.)

"It sounds to me like Clint ain't got no reason to blame hisself for Amare git'n away … and for what later happened to his wife," Dave reasoned.

"You're so right about that," Jim said in response as he massaged the muscles in the back of his neck. "No reason at all. It was just one of those things that no one had any real control over."

"I hear tell that Clint remarried," Geoff said. "Was it to that purty gal we met back in '92—when we was all headed up to Wes Baden's ranch?"

"Yup, it's the same gal," Jim replied.

"I remember her," Dave said thoughtfully. "She was the most handsome woman I ever did see. I'll never forget those big, dark brown eyes and that long, raven-colored hair."

"Me neither!" Geoff eagerly replied. "And I especially remember how well she filled out the top of that blouse she had on. She had the nicest—"

"Hey! Button it! That's our friend's wife you two are jawin' about. Show some respect," Jim said admonishingly.

"Sorry, Captain," Dave said.

"Yeah, me too," echoed Geoff.

No one spoke for the next couple of miles. Their thoughts were mostly on the upcoming campaign that would unfold at Four Peaks.

Titus Green, a tall, lanky twenty-two-year-old lad from Jerome, was the first to break the silence.

"Rangers, I'm git'n hungry. Is there a good place to eat in that ol' Payson town?"

"Yup, there is. Clint always recommends the Yellow Sun Café. His good friend, Betsy Lovemore, owns and operates the place," Jim replied as he considered his own hunger.

"Sounds good to me," Titus said.

"And, just so you know what we know, our ol' pal, Clint, gave the café its name," Jim added.

"How'd that come to be?" Titus asked.

"The café had only been open for a few days ... and

Betsy needed some ideas for a name. Well, along comes Clint. He glances about the café, notices all the yellow curtains and yellow tablecloths, and quickly blurts out a fit'n name. He told Betsy that the café looked real *sunny* to 'im," Jim explained.

"That makes sense to me," remarked Titus.

"Indeed. But there was a *second* reason behind Clint's choice of a name," continued Jim. "There's a café in Show Low called the Blue Moon—so Clint figured it would be rather catchy to call the one in Payson the Yellow Sun. Rather imaginative, don't you think?"

"I shore do think so," agreed Titus.

"It would appear that Clint has been blessed with an artistic way of thinking," Geoff said as he wiped the sweat from his neck again.

"Yup, I suppose. Well, now that everyone knows the history of the Yellow Sun Café, I think we had best lope these mounts of ours for a mile or two and see if we can make up a little time," Jim began, "'cause I'm git'n a bit hungry myself."

"Hey, Captain, ya got no monopoly on that miserable condition. I can just about smell the food uh cookin' from here!" Dave exclaimed.

* * * * *

It was around four o'clock when John Wheeler finally arrived at the Rim Shadow Ranch to look at the colts. Chip had all the two-year-olds cleaned up and ready to show.

Wheeler was quick to pick out a colt. He was familiar with Clint's sire, Liberty, and requested only to inspect the dam, which he was unfamiliar with. Chip brought out the mare for the prospective buyer to look over. After a few short minutes with her, Wheeler seemed satisfied that she was of good stock. He liked her gentle disposition as well.

"I think that colt I've selected will work out just fine," Wheeler said as he puffed on his pricey cigar.

"I'm delighted that you find him acceptable, Mr. Wheeler," Clint replied, with a smile forming on his face. "I reckon the only thing left for us to do is settle on a fair price."

"Yes, you're right, Mr. Wells," Wheeler said, still puffing on his cigar.

For the next several minutes, Wheeler and Clint went back and forth on the purchasing price of the colt. They finally came to an agreement. As Wheeler counted out his money, Clint prepared the bill of sale. A few minutes later, another satisfied customer rode off with his new colt in-tow.

"Praise the Lord! Now that's a *pretty penny!*" Clint exclaimed. "Chip, here's your share."

"Thanks, Mr. Wells!" Chip said, with a smile.

"You certainly earned it," Clint replied. "Now, let's get that three-year-old colt of mine out of his stall. I want to look him over real good. I have a feelin' that he's gonna see some major miles pass under his belly in the next few days."

"What's up, Mr. Wells?" Chip asked.

"It looks like I'll be hit'n the trail for a few days to assist the rangers with a situation south of here."

"What 'bout yer obligations here, sir?"

"Well, young man, it looks like *you* are gonna get to be the boss around here for a few days."

"Me! Why, I ain't ever been the boss of anything in

my whole life. Ya really trust me to handle things 'round here?"

"Chip, if I didn't think you could handle it, I wouldn't ride off and leave it in your hands," Clint quickly replied.

"Well, ya know I'll do my best, Mr. Wells. I'll make ya proud of me—I promise."

"I don't doubt that one bit," Clint said, patting his man on the back as they walked to the barn to retrieve the colt. "You'll do just fine, Chip."

Several minutes later, Clint was leading the energetic colt out of the barn and into the bright sunlight. The colt's ebony coat glimmered in the sun's rays.

"Boy, he's shore a beauty!" Chip exclaimed.

"Yes, indeed he is," agreed Clint. "Almost a spit'n image of Liberty. One day, he'll take over the breedin' duties from his ol' daddy."

"How old *is* Liberty, Mr. Wells?"

"He's eleven years old now," Clint replied, shaking his head in disbelief. "Where has the time gone?"

"Liberty is as 'fit-as-a-fiddle' as far as I can tell," Chip remarked. "I think, Mr. Wells, he'll be with ya for a long, long time."

"I hope you're right, son," Clint replied.

Clint looked over his colt carefully from head to tail. He especially checked the hooves for cracks, obstructions, and loose shoes. Everything looked fine.

"Chip," Clint began, "how would you like to take Apache out for a short ride? He could use some exercise."

"Huh? Are ya bein' serious with me, Mr. Wells?" Chip responded in utter disbelief.

"Wait here, while I get the tack," Clint said as he handed the lead rope to Chip and walked back to the barn.

Ten minutes later, Chip was trotting briskly down the lane toward the main road. He had never in his entire life been atop a horse as fine as this one. He was thrilled beyond words. One day he hoped to have a horse like this for his very own.

Clint watched as the young rider disappeared from his sight. He knew he was placing a lot of responsibility on the young man, but a quiet voice in his head told him that it was going to work out just fine. Clint didn't have to ask from where the heartening voice came. He knew it was from God.

Clint just hoped that he wouldn't be away too many days. The workload at the ranch could be overwhelming at times. Chip would probably be needed at the Double Creek Ranch as well—to assist with the stagecoach duties. Clint planned to speak with Robert and see if Dusty Rhodes would be available to fill that slot for a few days. Dusty and his father, Charlie, worked for Robert as cowpunchers. Charlie was also Robert's foreman. The father and son team had been with Robert for many years.

Thirty minutes later, Chip rode up to the corral. He had a big smile on his face that no one would be able to wipe away for a whole week—or longer.

Clint walked out to the corral to greet him.

"From the look on your face, I'd venture to say that you enjoyed every minute of your time in the saddle," Clint commented, while grinning at the bright-faced lad before him.

"Ya'd be right, Mr. Wells!" Chip responded exuberantly as he patted Apache on the neck. "What a horse!"

"I'm glad you and Apache got along so well. So, I'm

going to assume that he didn't give you any trouble to speak of," Clint said.

There was a very brief pause.

"My assumption is correct—right?" Clint asked, while "fishing" for some feedback from the youthful wrangler.

"No trouble at all, sir!" Chip readily answered as he dismounted. "He was well-mannered."

"I'm glad to hear it. Perhaps you'll get to ride Apache again in the near future," Clint announced as he turned about and walked back to the barn.

Chip led the spirited animal to the barn and busied himself with unsaddling the colt and wiping him down before giving him some water to drink. Soon, the colt was back in his stall, munching on some well-deserved oats.

Chip thought to himself: *Life is good here at the Rim Shadow Ranch.*

Chapter Two

It was nearly five o'clock when Captain O'Bryan and his three men rode into Payson. They dropped off their horses at the livery stable and made their way to the town marshal's office. When Jim and his rangers walked through the door, a young deputy quickly rose from his chair and greeted them.

"Welcome to Payson. I'm Kip Jones—Mike's deputy. We've been expectin' ya."

"Thanks. I'm Captain Jim O'Bryan," he said as he extended his hand in friendship. "Allow me to introduce my companions."

Jim completed the introductions and quickly surveyed the room. It appeared that the young deputy was alone.

"Where's Mike?" Jim wanted to know.

"He's gone home to eat dinner," Kip answered. "He said he might come back later."

"That's fine," Jim said. "We'll check back with you—*after* we've cleaned up and had our dinner."

"If he shows up later, I'll let 'im know that y'all are in town," Kip promised.

The rangers left the office and headed for the two-story Cedar Grove Hotel. A few minutes later they were in their rooms getting cleaned up for dinner.

An hour soon passed by the time the rangers met in the lobby of the hotel.

"What ya gonna order at the café, Dave?" Geoff asked, addressing his long-time friend.

"I don't have a clue, Geoff."

Jim, who had been discussing business with the hotel clerk, joined the conversation. "Gentlemen, may I suggest the fried chicken? Clint said it was the best he ever ate."

"I haven't tasted good fried chicken in a long time," Dave confessed, while smacking his lips. "An' I want a heapin' pile o' mashed potatoes sit'n right next to all that mouth-watering chicken."

"Oh yeah, that do sound good," agreed Geoff.

"Well, let's stop chewin' on our tongues and get over to the Yellow Sun Café and start chompin' down on some fryers," Jim light-heartedly commanded.

"Yes, sir, Captain. That's one order I won't hesitate to follow," Titus replied as he hustled out the hotel door ahead of the others.

* * * * *

By buggy, it was normally a direct fifteen-minute drive from Connie's store and café (located near the clear, cold, gurgling waters of Christopher Creek) to the Rim Shadow Ranch. Even though she closed the store and café at five o'clock, the decorative mantel clock at the ranch house would be chiming six bells by the time she arrived home. There were three key reasons for the delay in getting home: 1) It took anywhere from twenty to thirty minutes to clean up the café, 2) it took roughly fifteen minutes to swing by the Circle M Ranch and pick up little Lena from her temporary babysitter, Pamela Mayne, and 3) it took roughly ten minutes to drop off her aunt at the Double Creek Ranch.

Clint was standing on the porch when he heard the buggy approaching. As Connie pulled up in front of the hitching rail, he hurried over to the buggy and helped her disembark. The first thing Connie did—even before her feet touched the ground—was to give her husband a long, passionate kiss.

"Did you miss me, dear?" she asked, smiling.

"Only for the past ten hours."

"That's *all*?" she said as her lips protruded outward into a pout-like expression.

Seeing her expression, Clint hastily re-counted the hours that she had been away. "But that's how long you've been gone," he promptly replied.

"I know. I'm just teasing," she said as her expression quickly transformed into a pretty smile.

"I *knew* that," he shot back as he gave her another hearty hug and a quick peck on the lips.

Clint eagerly turned his attention to his daughter who was standing in the buggy. He stretched out his arms toward her. It was her signal to jump into his arms. And she did just that.

"Daddy!" she cried as soon as she was secure in his grip.

"Hi, sweetie!" he said as he gently squeezed his daughter in his burly arms.

Lena gave her father several big smooches on his cheeks as she hugged his neck.

"Clint, I'll wash up and start dinner while you tend to the horse and buggy," Connie said.

"Sounds like a perfect plan to me," he agreed as he turned and winked at his wife.

"Come on, sweetie. Let's get Daddy's dinner ready," Connie said as she stretched out her arms to retrieve Lena from her father's grip.

Connie and Lena entered the house.

Clint walked the horse to the barn with the buggy still attached. As soon as the buggy was properly positioned inside the barn, Clint unhitched the mare and took care of her needs. She was placed in a stall at the far end of the barn—a necessary safe distance from Apache.

Thirty minutes had elapsed by the time Clint headed for the house—with Chip following close at his heels. He could already smell dinner cooking. Connie was a very good cook. For years she had worked at Ma Thurman's café in Corydon, Indiana, as a waitress and cook before moving to Arizona.

Now thirty-one, and as lovely as ever, Connie was twenty-seven years old when Clint first laid eyes on her. He thought married life agreed with her. To him, she seemed happy. There was no doubt in Clint's mind that she made *him* very happy. She wasn't the "live wire" that Lisa had been, but she had all the other desired qualities of a first-rate companion. If pushed, Clint would probably confess that Connie was much more refined than Lisa. And that would be a correct assessment.

Connie was indeed happy with her marriage to Clint. She loved her husband more than anything in the world.

However, she sorely hated it that his first wife had died at the hands of an outlaw. She had liked Lisa a lot. They had been the best of friends.

Clint and Connie realized a long time ago that God ultimately controls the destiny of each and every person He creates, and that their marriage was a part of His plan. It was now up to them to make the very best of it. And, it was especially good for Lena to have a mother in the home again to teach her all those things that every young girl needs to learn as they're growing up—things that a father isn't always qualified to handle. Connie was fully aware that Clint knew more about raising horses than he did about raising a daughter.

There was a lot of small talk over dinner. Connie apprised Clint of her day at the store. She reported that sales were up from the previous week at the café *and* the mercantile store. Lastly, she disclosed that she had hired a new waitress.

"She's rather young—just sixteen. But she's incredibly eager to learn. And so far, she's done a first-rate job," Connie reported as she reached over to wipe food from Lena's chin.

"How long has she been with you?"

"This was her third day."

"Where did you find her?"

"Almost in our own backyard. It's your and Lisa's niece, Maree."

"Aw, you don't say? Well, that's wonderful!"

"So, my husband, you approve?"

"Certainly. I think she will be a great asset to you. I can remember when she, her brother, and her mother used to live here at the ranch. That girl helped me out many a time with the horses. She's a very tireless worker."

And she's cute, too, Chip instantly thought.

Chip was hopelessly attracted to Maree. And, unknown to him, Maree felt the same way about him. Her visits to the Rim Shadow Ranch had become purposely more frequent over the past two months. Clint and Connie, it seemed, were oblivious to the attraction that was rapidly developing between their niece and their ranch hand.

"I agree, Clint. She *is* an asset," Connie said.

"How did her mother and stepfather react to her takin' a job at the café?" Clint asked.

"Jenny is very pleased. I told her I might even hire her son as a store clerk when he gets older."

"What was Jenny's reaction to that?"

"She said Kris would have to remain at their ranch and help her husband with the overwhelming number of chores they have there. I told her that I completely understood."

"I can certainly relate to that. I'm sure Dusty would hate to lose the help of his stepson—even if the boy is only fourteen years old at the moment."

There was a brief lull in the conversation as the bowls were passed around for second helpings. Clint and Chip never passed up filling their plates a second time—or a third.

"So, my husband, what's new with you?" Connie asked as she wiped another glob of food from Lena's chin. "Anything exciting happen today?"

"Sold a colt. Got a good price for him too."

"Oh, Clint, that's wonderful! Please, tell me all about it."

Clint spent the next several minutes going over the details of the sale. He gave a lot of credit to Chip for getting the colt ready to present. Chip beamed as Clint spoke about his involvement. Connie was more than pleased with the selling price.

As soon as dinner was over, Chip placed his soiled dishes in the sink and excused himself. "It was a grand meal, ma'am—as always," he said.

"Thank you, Chip. I'm glad you enjoy my style of cooking. I'll see you at breakfast. Goodnight."

"Goodnight, ma'am."

Clint removed his daughter from the table and began cleaning her up. She was a messy eater. "I'll get this little one ready for bed and come back and help you with the dishes," he said.

"No rush. Take your time," she replied as she finished her coffee. "I promise not to start without you."

Clint's mind suddenly focused on that letter from Major Williamson. He knew he couldn't hold off any longer bringing it up. *It's gonna ruin the rest of my evening,* he thought.

"Connie, I … uh … have somethin' to discuss with you later. It's a rather … uh … major situation," he admitted as he slipped out of the room with Lena.

Connie suddenly felt her stomach turn over. When her husband stammered his words, she knew she wasn't going to like what he had to say. She rose from the table and followed him into Lena's bedroom.

"Clint, tell me what's going on?" she asked as she placed her hand on his shoulder.

"I got a letter today—from Williamson," he said, while deliberately avoiding eye contact.

"Oh, no. That can't be good," she sighed.

"I don't deny that. The only bright spot in his letter was the fact that he has gotten married to a nice lady by the name of Linda. He said we would like her a lot."

"I'm happy for *him*, but right now I don't think I'm going to be happy for *me*. So *where* are you off to this time?" she asked, with a note of despair in her voice.

"*Four Peaks*. It's not too far from Phoenix. To the east I think. It's gonna be a large-scale campaign ... and perhaps the last one for the rangers."

"What do you mean by—*last?*"

"Tom says that the territorial governor's political advisors have convinced him to disband the rangers at the end of the year."

"Well, I wish the governor had disbanded the rangers *yesterday*. Then my man wouldn't be riding off into another dangerous situation."

"Yes, my love, I agree. The letter is on my desk. I'd like for you to read it," Clint concluded as he pulled Lena's nightgown on over her head.

Connie left the bedroom and retrieved the letter from the desk. She returned to the kitchen and sat down at the table. Before opening the letter, she stared at it for a long moment. She sighed deeply as she pulled the letter from its envelope.

She read it, not once, but twice. It was not the kind of news she wanted her husband to receive. She thought back to the time, four years ago, when he was nearly killed at the Mogollon Rim Ranch by Frank Carver; and to the time, two years later, when an outlaw that he was chasing killed his first wife, Lisa. *And now this horrible deal is dropped into his lap!* Connie muttered to herself.

Connie folded the letter up and slid it back into the envelope. At that moment Clint approached her and sat down at the table. He immediately reached across the table, pulled the envelope from her hand, and laid it aside. Then, he reached back across the table and took both of her hands into his. He could not help but notice a tear forming in her left eye.

"I don't know what to say, Connie."

"There's really nothing you *can* say, Clint," she replied as the tear broke free, ran down her cheek, and stopped at the corner of her mouth.

"I know you're right about that," he said as he continued to hold her hands.

After a brief moment, Connie pulled her hands free, wiped the tear from her face, and stood up. "I'll make some more coffee, and then, we'll go out on the porch for some fresh air," she announced as she attempted to muster up a smile.

"Yes, that would be nice. I'll fetch your wrap. It's git'n a heap colder now when the sun goes down. It won't be too long before the first snow," he said, in an attempt to break the tension inside the room.

Clint retrieved Connie's shawl, and a light jacket for himself. At 6,000 feet above sea level, the warm days of summer faded fast during the month of October. Clint was glad that he already had most of the firewood they would need for the stove stacked on the back porch. A good friend, Owen Clements, who lived a few miles to the west, had promised Clint an additional wagonload of firewood by the end of the month.

Minutes later, Connie approached her husband and handed him a large mug filled with fresh, black coffee. He clutched it firmly in his hands as he escorted his wife to the front porch.

"Ooh, it *is* chilly out here!" she commented as they each sought out a rocking chair.

"Yep, and it ain't gonna get any better until next spring," he replied as they both sat down.

"*Isn't*," she corrected.

"That's what I said—*ain't*," he teased as he leaned

forward in his rocking chair and gave her a kiss on the cheek.

"What was *that* for?"

"For being you."

"And just who am I to you?"

"Everything a man could want in a woman."

"Are you sure of that?"

"There's not the slightest doubt in my mind."

Clint and Connie sat and rocked in their individual chairs for several minutes, sipping coffee, and saying nothing to each other. Only the creaking sound of the wooden rockers broke the silence, that is, until Connie finally spoke.

"When do you leave?"

"Not sure. Jim O'Bryan will be here tomorrow. He is supposed to have all the details. I'm guessin' it will be very soon—perhaps in the next two days."

"What about the ranch?"

"I believe Chip can handle things around here just fine. He's very dependable, you know."

Clint paused, then said, "I'll let Robert know I'm going away for a spell. I don't think he will mind checkin' on you and Lena while I'm away."

"Not at all. My brother would be more than glad to do that for us," she declared. "However, he won't like the fact that you're leaving again—for parts unknown. He worries about you when you're off chasing outlaws—just like I do."

"He does?" Clint said, his eyebrows rising slightly. "I didn't know that."

"Of course. You are his best friend."

"He is certainly mine ... uh ... outside of you, of course," he said, with the best of diplomacy.

"That's good to know," she said, smiling.

"I'm ready to go inside if you are?" he said.

"Yes, I'm a bit chilled. I need to get warm," she confessed as they were both rising from their chairs.

"If you'll allow me, ma'am, perhaps I could be the primary source of your warmth?" he said, grinning. "*Warmth* is my middle name."

"Hmmm, I rather believe you could be the perfect source of warmth I'm looking for," she coyly answered. "Are you up to it, ol' timer?"

"Well, that depends. Just how *warm* do you need to get?" he asked, while putting his arm around her shoulders.

"*Very*," she said as she leaned into him.

"Hmmm, it sounds like this ol' cowboy is gonna be real busy for the next couple of hours. And I won't complain one bit."

Connie blushed. She could already feel the warmth building in her body in anticipation of being with her husband in an intimate way.

"*Complain*?" Connie finally responded as she pinched his arm. "I *guarantee* that you'll have nothing to complain about."

It was Clint's turn to blush. He knew from past experience that she would make good that guarantee.

No doubt—a *very* warm night was in the forecast.

* * * * *

Captain O'Bryan and his men were walking toward the town marshal's office. Their meal at the Yellow Sun Café had been the best that any of them had eaten in a very long time.

"No wonder Clint recommends that place," Titus remarked as he wiped a gravy stain from his already soiled shirt. "It was scrumptious."

"I'm stuffed," Geoff said. "I should not have had that second big piece o' pumpkin pie."

At the marshal's office, they learned from the deputy that Mike hadn't returned to town.

"We'll stop by in the morning," Jim said as he led his team of rangers out the door.

They went directly to the hotel.

Jim paused as he prepared to unlock the door to his and Dave's shared room.

"Gentlemen," he began, "we'll meet downstairs at six o'clock in the mornin'. Y'all get some rest. We've got another long ride tomorrow."

"I don't know if my tailbone can take another long day in the saddle," complained the young Titus Green.

"Buck up, kid," Geoff quipped as he stepped into his room. "When ya've straddled leather as long as I have, ya will toughen up a bit."

"Pardon me, sir, if I don't cherish the thought of possessin' a callused tailbone," Titus readily countered as he followed Geoff into the room they were sharing.

* * * * *

In a box canyon fifty-five miles south of Payson, a large group of men were settling into their bedrolls for the night. The only thing between them and the stars above were several large, makeshift lean-tos. Two campfires were burning brightly just a few feet away from these primitive shelters. As these men inside the canyon prepared to sleep, two other men outside the canyon would be fighting to stay awake for the next few hours. As sentries, their job was to protect the entrance to the canyon.

These sentries had a small campfire glowing nearby for warmth. Four hours from now, two other men would relieve them. Night and day, this routine had been repeated over and over for the past several months. Wild Burro Canyon had become a stronghold to a large band of merciless outlaws.

From their hidden base camp, these outlaws were making daily raids on the surrounding territory. No person or property was off limits in their book of rules. This day had been no different. A dozen men from this group had already made an early morning raid on a nearby ranch—making off with three calves. One of those calves quickly ended up as the "special-of-the-day" on the camp's menu. The other two calves would probably not survive the week.

Two days ago, a feed store had been their primary target. The outlaws made off with enough horse feed to last about a week. Though a fresh-water spring was not far from the canyon, there was little or no grass or anything else suitable for the horses to eat. Most of the vegetation consisted of cacti and scrub brush.

Butch Kantrell was the hardcore leader of this incorrigible group of men. With the support of his two lieutenants, he was able to maintain order in the camp. Earlier in the day, he informed his lieutenants that it was his plan to lead them out of the canyon in the not-so-distant future and find "greener pastures" from which they could launch their raids.

Little did the outlaw leader know that others were coming to lead him and his men out of the canyon—in handcuffs.

Chapter Three

Wednesday, October 7th.

The sun was slowly climbing above the eastern horizon bigger and brighter and more orange than Clint had ever remembered seeing it. He wondered if it was a good omen or a bad omen of things to come. He prayed for the former.

I wonder when Jim O'Bryan will be here? Clint asked himself.

He hoped it would be later in the day because he had much to do before riding off and leaving the place in Chip's hands. One of the things he had to do was walk over to Robert's place and let him know what was happening.

Clint walked to the bunkhouse and knocked on the door. A few seconds later, Chip opened the door. He was already dressed, except for his boots.

"Ready for breakfast?" Clint asked.

"Yes, sir. Just be a minute."

"I'll see you at the house," Clint concluded.

Clint did an about-face and walked briskly back to the house. As he entered the living room, he spotted Connie standing in the kitchen near the stove. She was preparing to heat up the skillet and fry some bacon and eggs.

"Good morning!" she said, rather vibrantly.

"And a good mornin' to you, sweet lady!"

"Are you ready for breakfast?" she asked.

"Yes, indeed. And Chip is up and dressed. He should be here in a few minutes."

"Coffee's ready," she said as she placed three large mugs on the kitchen countertop.

"Did you sleep well last night, my love?" he asked as he slipped up behind her and put his arms around her torso. "And, were you *warm* enough?"

"Ummm, yes, to both questions," she answered, demurely. "Thank you so very much. And what about you, cowboy, were you *warm* enough last night?"

"It's safe to say that I won't ever need to put an extra log on the fire when I'm layin' next to you," he replied in an attempt to express his great satisfaction with the past night's lovemaking.

"Well, I'm glad you find me more useful than a fireplace log," she teased.

Connie spun about in his arms and planted a big kiss on his lips. "And, my big hunk of a cowboy, I've got a very strong feeling that I may require a good *warming* again tonight."

"Is that so?" he said, grinning.

Just as they were about to lock lips again, a knock came at the door. It was Chip.

"I'm so glad he always knocks first," she said.

"That's for sure," he quipped as he hastily stepped away from Connie. "I'd certainly hate for him to catch us misbehavin' around here."

"Come in, Chip!" Connie shouted.

Chip entered the house, removed his hat, and walked into the kitchen. Clint poured him a mug of coffee and invited him to sit at the table. Chip took the coffee and sat down—placing his hat under the high-back chair.

"Are you feelin' okay this mornin', son?" Clint asked.

"Yes, sir," Chip began, "doin' just fine. But I didn't sleep so well. Was thinkin' 'bout yer bein' away and me tryin' to fill yer shoes for a few days."

Sensing that Clint and Chip needed a moment to themselves, Connie excused herself.

"I'll go get Lena up," Connie said as she walked out of the kitchen. "Keep an eye on the skillet."

"Can do," Clint said.

Clint and Chip talked for several minutes. Clint reassured the young cowboy that everything would be just fine. It seemed to help—a lot.

Connie returned with Lena who was still in her nightgown. The young girl gave her father a kiss and took her usual place at the table. Clint reached over and placed a bib about her neck.

Connie finished preparing and serving each plate of food. Chip gave the blessing as soon as she was seated at the table. Clint's departure was not discussed during the meal. There would be time enough for that conversation later in the day.

After breakfast, Chip went out to the barn to prepare the buggy for Connie. Meanwhile, Clint walked over to Robert's place to inform him of the new campaign he was about to embark upon. It was just a five-minute walk through the woods on a well-worn trail.

Clint soon learned that Connie was right in her

assessment of her brother's attitude toward his riding off to chase outlaws again. Robert wasn't very pleased about the news. However, when Clint informed him that it was probably the last ride for the rangers, he was extremely pleased.

"I pray to God that it is so," he said to Clint.

They also discussed the stagecoach duties, and whether or not Chip would be involved. Robert said he would speak to Dusty Rhodes about taking over those duties for a few days.

* * * * *

It was around four o'clock when Captain O'Bryan and his men arrived at the Rim Shadow Ranch. Clint was at the corral when he heard them riding up the lane. Chip was away, exercising one of the mares.

"*¡Buenos tardes, mi amigos!*" Clint shouted from the far side of the corral.

"And a good afternoon to you, too, my friend," Jim said as he rode closer to where Clint stood.

"Climb down and make yourselves at home," Clint said, cheerfully. "I'm sure you've had a long ride from Fort Verde."

"Actually, Clint, just from Payson. We spent the night there," Jim explained.

Handshakes were exchanged. The new man, Titus Green, was introduced to Clint. "Glad to have you aboard. I hope these ol' pards of mine haven't been too rough on you?"

"No, sir," Titus answered, "not at all."

"That's good."

Clint was glad to see his friends again—and told them

so. He quickly suggested that they get their horses un-saddled and cared for, stake a claim to some beds in the bunkhouse, and then join him later on the porch for some apple cider. Without any hesitation, they followed his directive to the letter.

Clint was the first to speak when they finally joined him on the porch. "Gentlemen, Connie will be preparin' a hearty meal for y'all when she gets home. I hope you're able to ward off starvation for an hour or two?"

"Not a problem, Clint. Just sit'n down to a home-cooked meal will be nothin' short of pure pleasure," Jim said with a smile.

"Here's a pitcher of apple cider and some glasses. Help yourselves," Clint said.

"Ya are a fortunate man, Clint. Ya shore got a nice place here," Titus said as his eyes scanned the property.

"Yes, I certainly think so. God has richly blessed my life—though I hardly deserve it."

"Maybe one day I'll be so lucky," Titus added.

"I don't put much faith in *luck*, but I do believe in God's blessings and hard work," Clint countered.

"Uh ... yes ... of course," Titus said, looking a bit lost for a proper response. It was rather obvious to the other three rangers that Titus did not share Clint's faith in God.

Clint, uncomfortable with discussing his personal as-sets, quickly changed the subject. "While we're awaitin' Connie's arrival—why don't y'all fill me in on this deal we are ridin' into."

"Of course, Clint, I'd be glad to do that," Jim said, clearing his throat.

Besides the rocking chair Clint was occupying, there were three more. The veteran rangers quickly filled them.

Titus seated himself atop the porch railing. As soon as everyone was settled in, Jim began to explain the upcoming campaign as best as he understood it.

"This is gonna be big, Clint. We are lookin' at a tough bunch of *hombres*. There may be as many as forty to fifty outlaws hidin' near the base of Four Peaks.

"This bunch has held up stagecoaches, robbed and killed innocent civilians, rustled cattle and sheep, and even held up the Southern Pacific train near Maricopa.

"The governor is askin' that all law enforcement agencies get involved in this campaign. And, as far as I know, there'll be a large turnout of lawmen." Jim briefly hesitated. "Well, at least I hope so."

"*When* do we ride? And *where* are we to meet?" Clint readily inquired.

"We'll leave tomorrow morning," Jim answered. "The rendezvous point is near the east bank of Sycamore Creek—at a place called Sugar Loaf Mountain. We're to assemble there by Saturday afternoon."

"So, we've got three whole days to get there?"

"That's right, Clint. It's roughly seventy miles from here," Jim surmised. "That should give us plenty of time."

"Well, sir, I invested a couple of hours today organizing my things for the trip. I see that y'all brought a packhorse with some supplies. Is there anything I can contribute?" Clint asked.

"Just be shore ya got plenty o' ammo," Dave cautioned, "'cause there's gonna be a lot of lead flyin' about. Them *yahoos* ain't gonna wave no white flag."

"It's too bad we don't have Major Williamson with us on this campaign," Jim commented.

"And, Will Clowers," Dave added.

"Right, ya are!" Geoff smartly agreed.

"We had a chance this mornin' to talk with the town marshal in Payson," Jim began, "and he's goin' with us."

Clint, with a hint of surprise in his voice, said, "You talkin' about Mike Chandler?"

"He'd be the one," Jim answered. "He's got a new deputy—so he's free to join us."

"Why not send the new deputy?" Clint asked.

"Mike doesn't feel like his deputy has enough experience to bite off somethin' this big," Jim explained. "He thinks the *greenhorn* would just get himself killed."

"Yeah, that makes sense," Clint agreed.

"We've got two more men comin' from Prescott. They are veteran rangers ... and will be a big help to us. Geoff and Dave met 'em last year," Jim added.

"That's certainly good news," Clint replied. "They got names? I might know one of 'em."

"Chino Watson and Dewey Loomis," Dave readily responded before Jim could answer.

"Can't say I know 'em," Clint said, shaking his head. "I once knew a man by the name of Goodwin."

"He's still over there," affirmed Geoff. "He's git'n up in years though. Reckon he'll be retirin' soon."

"He won't have to retire. Word is, the rangers are bein' disbanded at the end of the year," declared Clint, repeating the words he had read in Williamson's letter.

"Yeah, we heard that, too. But we are hopin' it won't happen," Geoff replied, frowning. "Seems they don't appreciate us. It's a slap in the face for shore."

"What will y'all do if it *does* happen?" Clint asked, hoping he wouldn't generate any anguish.

"I'm not sure," Jim answered. "Maybe head out to the coast and soak my feet in the ocean. I hear San Diego is a lovely place. And, it's always a pleasant seventy-five degrees—or so I've been told."

"I always wanted to see Colorado," Dave said.

"What about you, Geoff?" Clint asked.

"Oh, I don't know. Maybe head back east. I got family in Dayton that I haven't seen in years. Might be nice to reacquaint myself with some of 'em."

"What are your plans, Titus?" Clint asked in an effort to draw the new man into the conversation.

"Haven't given it much thought," Titus replied as he rubbed his chin in contemplation.

"Well, you're still a young man. You've got a lot of years ahead of you. I'm sure, in time, you'll decide what to do with the rest of your life," Jim supposed.

At that moment, Chip Bowman returned from his ride. He waved at the men on the porch and went straight to the barn to unsaddle, rub down, and water the mare before turning her out into the corral.

"Who's that?" Dave asked.

"He's my new wrangler. And, he really knows horses. I'm blessed to have him workin' for me."

"Will he be takin' care of things while you are away?" Jim asked.

"Yep. I think he can handle things just fine."

The rangers continued to chat while they waited for Chip to finish with the mare. They halted their conversation when Chip, at last, walked up to the porch. Clint made the proper introductions as handshakes were exchanged. With Chip sitting close by on the porch steps, the conversation continued—mostly just small talk. Chip listened intently.

Just as the mantel clock's chime began counting to

six, a horse could be heard trotting up the lane. It was Connie. She maneuvered the black buggy around the west perimeter of the courtyard and halted the rig perfectly in front of the porch steps.

Chip leaped from the steps and grabbed the mare's halter to steady her. Meanwhile, Clint rose quickly from his rocking chair and hastily made his way to the buggy to assist his wife and daughter.

"Thank you, Clint," she said with graciousness as he helped her down. She then glanced over his shoulder at the group of staring eyes on the porch.

Feeling somewhat uncomfortable in front of an audience, Connie merely gave her husband a quick kiss on the cheek. Anything of a passionate nature would have to wait for a private moment.

"Hi, Daddy!" Lena shouted with excitement. Then she leaped from the buggy into his outstretched arms. Clint gave his daughter a hug and a quick kiss on the cheek.

Clint, while carrying his daughter, escorted his wife up the steps to the porch. He promptly began with the introductions. The rangers came to their feet immediately and removed their hats in the presence of Connie. She recognized Jim right off, but she had not seen Dave and Geoff for nearly four years and scarcely remembered them.

"When did you arrive?" she asked.

"As near as I can tell, ma'am, I reckon we've been here a couple of hours," Jim kindly replied.

"I'm assuming my dear husband has seen to your accommodations—right?"

"Yes, ma'am, he has," Jim answered. "We already have our things stored in the bunkhouse."

"Well, I'll see to it that you all get properly fed while you are here at the ranch."

Dave nodded. "That's most kind, ma'am."

"It shouldn't be too long before dinner is ready," she concluded as she excused herself. With Lena in-tow, she entered the house.

The men donned their hats, reseated themselves, and picked up their conversation where they had left off.

By seven-thirty, everyone had eaten their fill. To Connie's surprise and pleasure, the rangers even washed the dishes before retiring to the front porch for more conversation. By nine o'clock, they had gone to the bunkhouse to sleep. Chip remained behind a few minutes longer to chat with Clint. He received some additional last-minute instructions from his boss. Chip carefully noted each item.

As soon as Chip departed for the bunkhouse, Connie came outside and stood next to her husband. "Honey, are you ready to come in?"

"Yes, most definitely. It's git'n rather chilly out here. I dread the arrival of winter."

"I put Lena in her bed a few minutes ago. She had fallen asleep on the sofa while you were out here talking with the rangers."

"She did?"

Clint suddenly felt sad that he didn't get to say goodnight to his daughter. He went directly to her bedroom and leaned down and gave her a kiss on the forehead. She stirred slightly but did not wake up. He stood over her bed in an attitude of prayer for several minutes.

He then walked into his own bedroom to find his beautiful wife standing near the dressing table wearing nothing but a dark red, knee-length nightgown. It was sleeveless, and cut very low in the front. She looked absolutely ravishing. She had unpinned her long black hair, allowing it to hang freely over her shoulders and down across her breasts. The tips of her hair nearly reached her waist.

"Wow! You're takin' my breath away," Clint said as his eyes nearly popped out of their sockets.

Connie could not believe her boldness. She had never worn anything this seductive in her entire life.

"Why, thank you, dear. I'm so glad that you approve."

"Where did you find a gown like that?"

"I ordered the material from one of my store catalogs, and then, I sewed it myself from a pattern. And, I confess, I took some liberties with the pattern—as you can see," she said, while lifting the hem of the gown higher to expose her shapely thighs.

"And how! I'll be back as soon as I clean up," he said as he sped out of the room.

"I'll be waiting!" she softly called out.

Ten minutes later, Clint crawled into bed next to his wife. She snuggled up close to him and threw her right arm across his bare torso. That was quickly followed by a series of kisses that pelted his face.

"Ummm, you smell real nice," he said as he sniffed about her neck. "And, honey, you certainly know how to get my undivided attention."

"Well, that sounds *very* promising," she said, while rubbing her hand softly across his bare chest. "So, pour on the attention, cowboy. The clock is running."

"With great pleasure, ma'am."

It wasn't very long before Clint and Connie were deeply engrossed in their lovemaking. They both knew this would be their last night together for sometime—and they meant to make the most of it. Thoughts about tomorrow were put aside. The *present* was all that mattered to them at this moment.

As for created beings, the future is an unknown part of life. Only God has the privilege of knowing what the future holds. Clint, better than anyone else, realized that. He had already lost someone very dear to him.

Clint loved, respected, and appreciated Connie. He would lay down his life for her if necessary. She was better to him than he felt he deserved. God, he truly believed, had blessed him beyond measure. He had a devoted and loving wife, a beautiful child, great friends, and a prosperous ranch.

It was nearly eleven o'clock by the time Clint and Connie relaxed their bodies. It was now time to enjoy the *afterglow* of their lovemaking. They soon fell asleep in the arms of the other.

* * * * *

Before going to bed, Major Tom Williamson and his wife, Linda, had prayed for the rangers' success at Four Peaks.

Now, as he lay in bed, he wished, in a nostalgic way, that he could be with them. His mind drifted back to the days when he rode with each of them. They had shared many an exciting adventure together.

He wondered how well Clint would cope with this new campaign. He knew it took a lot of intestinal fortitude for Clint to get back into the game. He was proud of his friend, and was overjoyed to know that the former Texas

Ranger would be riding side-by-side again with his fellow Arizona lawmen.

Tom knew that Jim and Clint had complimented each other on all previous campaigns. They were both born leaders. Jim deserved to be a captain, and Tom was delighted that Jim's promotion had come through. He also knew that Clint certainly deserved to be a captain, as well.

Tom's mind started to drift. Sleep finally overtook him.

* * * * *

At the bunkhouse, the rangers chatted away until the eleventh hour. They covered a wide variety of topics. The chief topic was the perilous situation at Four Peaks. Predictable anxiety floated about the room—especially in the mind of Titus Green. This would be his first major outing with the rangers, and he dearly hoped that he was up to the task.

With luck, I'll be okay, Titus thought.

Before calling it a night, the conversation turned to Clint, and the ranch he had built for himself and his family.

"I'm so glad that Clint is goin' with us on this campaign," Jim said. "He's one of the best lawmen in the territory ... and he's a crack shot."

"It's pretty obvious that his wife isn't too pleased 'bout his ridin' out with us," Dave noted. "She hadn't much to say during dinner."

"I'm guessing you're right 'bout that," Jim agreed. "Reckon I don't blame her none."

Geoff quickly changed the subject. "This shore is one nice ranch," he rightly commented. "Never seen another like it in these parts."

"He's certainly got some fine horse flesh in them cor-rals," Jim commented. "A man would be blessed to own one of 'em mares."

"Say, what did y'all think of that young black stallion in the barn?" Titus asked. "Now that is some fine horse, huh?"

"I ain't never in my life seen a finer horse—except maybe Clint's older stallion, Liberty," Geoff remarked. "There was a time when that big chestnut could outrun any horse in the territory."

"Yep," agreed Dave, "and probably still can."

"This place makes me want to run out and buy a place of my own," Jim said with a sigh. "And maybe get married, too."

"I'll say one thing more—that wife of his shore can cook," Titus commented. "I'd be twenty pounds heavier if I ate here every single day."

"It wouldn't hurt ya none if ya did gain a pound or two," Geoff piped up. "Ya don't weigh a hundred pounds soakin' wet."

"I'll have ya know that I weigh nearly one hundred forty pounds," Titus countered.

"Ol' Geoff here—well, he's got to weigh in at over two hundred pounds," Dave guessed.

"Two twenty," Geoff fired back. "And it's all *muscle*."

"Yeah, right!" Jim quipped, laughing.

"At least I won't be blown off my horse in a wind storm like the rest of ya," countered Geoff, in an attempt to push back against the ribbing.

"Okay, men," Jim began, "it's time to sleep."

One wall away, in the foreman's section of the bunk-house, Chip Bowman was wide-awake. Though the rangers' voices had been somewhat muffled by the four-inch-thick insulated wall, he had, nonetheless, managed to overhear some of their conversation.

He was in agreement as to how nice things were at Rim Shadow Ranch. He felt blessed to be in the employ of Clint Wells. And at the moment, he was thinking about Clint's departure, and how he was going to cope with all the chores. He was glad that he had gained a lot of experience working with his boss over the past few months.

Maybe it won't be too bad, he thought.

Suddenly, and with ease, Chip's mind went from thoughts of his boss leaving the ranch, for an undetermined amount of time, to sweet thoughts of the lovely Maree Reavis. She was sixteen, and he was twenty. He couldn't decide if that was good or bad. And to complicate things, she was his boss's niece.

She seems very mature for her age, he thought.

For several minutes, tender thoughts of Maree lingered in his mind. He wondered if he would ever muster up the courage to tell her how he felt about her. The thing that scared him most was how his boss would react if he found out.

As the clock crept toward mid-night, Chip's mind began to cloud over. His various thoughts started to collide with each other. He finally gave in to sleep.

* * * * *

Two hours into her sleep, Connie began to stir. She opened her eyes at looked over at her slumbering husband. She felt the need to wake him, but could not make up her mind to do so. Since he had to ride out very early in the morning, she knew that he would need as much rest as possible.

Finally, after long fretful moments she leaned close to him and began to nibble at his ear as her hand explored his lower torso. In no time, she could feel his body responding to her tender touch.

Clint began to stir. He wasn't sure if he was dreaming or if what he was sensing was actually happening. He opened his eyes and looked into the face of his wife. He smiled.

Connie's request was simple. "I need you."

Clint drew his wife into his strong arms. He was overwhelmingly pleased by her request. He had no clue when she would be in his arms again. This was a sweet moment in time that he would not pass up for any reason. Besides, how could he, or any man for that matter, say "no" to a woman as splendid as this woman was. And she wanted *him*.

Chapter Four

Thursday, October 8th.

It was nearly six o'clock when Clint walked out onto the porch. The sun was still well below the eastern horizon. Only a faint glimmer of light was visible. And, the air was cold enough for Clint to see his breath fog as he exhaled. He was glad that he had donned his fleeced-lined denim jacket before coming outside.

As Clint walked toward the barn, he could hear voices coming from the main part of the bunkhouse. He assumed that the rangers were up and getting dressed. However, he did not see or hear any signs of activity coming from the private room at the south end of the bunkhouse. That was Chip's room—a room normally reserved for a ranch foreman.

At the barn, Clint led Apache from his stall and positioned him in the center of the barn's aisle. His colt was then secured between two ropes—one strung from each side of the aisle. He gathered together his tack and began saddling his colt. Being an experienced rider, Clint preferred a double-bridle for more precise control. He also used a martingale to prevent the colt from tossing his head. His saddle of choice was a double-rigged Texan. It was black—with a modest amount of silver adornment.

Fifteen minutes later, the colt was saddled, and the saddlebags were firmly secured to the rear skirt. The saddlebags contained an extra Colt .44-.40 caliber pistol and plenty of ammunition on one side, and his personal grooming items on the other side—plus a change of clothes.

The scabbard for his Model 1873 Winchester .44-.40 caliber rifle was secured to the right side of the saddle, with the open end facing rearward. His bedroll, canvas tarp, and rain slicker were the last items to be secured over the top of his saddlebags. He elected not to bring his knee-length duster coat. *My denim jacket should be enough*, he thought aloud.

Clint led his colt out of the barn and walked him to the hitching rail in front of the house. Apache was acting a bit unsettled. Clint patted his neck and talked softly to him. He quickly quieted down.

At that moment, Connie poked her head out the door. "Clint, is everyone up?"

"All except Chip. I'm about to roust him out of bed. He was dog-tired last night when he turned in."

"I'm certainly glad *you* weren't!" she said, seductively, as a playful smile slowly formed on her pretty face.

"Yeah, that makes *two* of us!" he said with a nod, followed by a sly grin.

"I'll start preparing breakfast," she said as she ducked back into the house. *Brrr*, she mumbled under her breath as she closed the door, *it's chilly this morning!*

Just as Clint was about to knock on Chip's door,

the four rangers filed out onto the bunkhouse's porch. Greetings were exchanged as the rangers strode to the barn to retrieve their horses and tack. Clint, meanwhile, began knocking on Chip's door. It took a minute, but the door finally opened.

"Rise and shine, son!"

"Y-yes, sir," he said, with eyes half open.

The sun was now glowing orange as Clint walked back to the house. It seemed colder to him *now* than it did thirty minutes earlier. He could still see his breath fog in the cold morning air. *Winter's uh comin' early this year*, he thought.

As Clint ascended the steps of his house, he inhaled deeply to capture all the aromas that were escaping from inside, such as, the coffee beans brewing, and the bacon frying in Connie's big iron skillet.

He walked into the kitchen and gave Connie a hug—and a very prolonged kiss on the lips. Then, he started kissing her neck and nibbling on her ear. He could sense her body responding. But, when his right hand moved from her waist to her left breast—she slammed on the brakes.

"Whoa, cowboy! Keep *that* up and you'll not get any breakfast. You and me will be much too busy in the bedroom cooking up something a lot more delightful," she said. "And, I'm thinking there's some rangers and a wrangler outside that won't take too kindly to missing a meal."

"You're so right," he said, laughing.

"Breakfast will be ready in about ten minutes. Go round them up, please."

"Shall I set the table first?"

"No. We are having our meal *buffet* style."

When Clint walked out onto the porch, he noticed that the rangers had their mounts ready to ride and were hitching them to the rails in front of the bunkhouse.

"Wash up, men! Breakfast will be served in ten minutes!" he shouted from the porch.

"Be right there, Clint!" Jim responded.

Breakfast was quite tasty, and everyone ate his or her fill. And, the rangers even pitched in and helped Connie clear the table. Clint was pleased that his guests were considerate of his wife.

Chip and the rangers thanked Connie for fixing their breakfast. Then, they all departed the house, except Clint. He remained behind to say his farewells to Connie and little Lena. It wasn't easy saying goodbye to them. Connie tried to be brave, but she broke down and cried. Clint did his best to comfort her. Lena hugged his neck tightly and was very reluctant to let go when he tried to hand her off to Connie.

"I'll be praying for you and the rangers," Connie promised. "I love you, Mr. Wells."

"I love you *more*, Mrs. Wells."

"That's not possible!"

"We'll argue that point when I get home."

She winked at him. "I'll look forward to it."

Clint slipped on his brown leather vest and denim jacket.

"Button your coat, dear," she said. "I don't want my man to get chilled."

"I will," he replied. "And if I *were* to get chilled?"

She blushed and gave him a big smile.

Clint returned the smile, and then he blew kisses to his wife and daughter as he grabbed his rifle and walked out the door. Once at his horse, he slipped the rifle into the well-oiled scabbard. Next, he extracted the fully loaded bandolier from the saddle horn and positioned it loosely across his body—from top right to lower left. He wore it that way because he did not want the bandolier interfering with the extraction of his Model 1878 Colt .44-.40 revolver from its holster.

Clint said his farewell to Chip and mounted up. He joined the rangers at the bunkhouse and waited for them to mount their horses. A few minutes later, everyone was ready to travel.

"Goodbye rangers!" Chip shouted. "And be careful!"

Clint turned about in his saddle and saw Connie on the porch holding Lena. They were both waving to him and blowing kisses. He waved back before following the rangers down the lane to the main road.

When they reached the main road—and were completely out of view of the house—Clint reached into his jacket pocket and retrieved the silver badge of an Arizona Ranger. He stared at it for a moment, polished it on his jacket sleeve, and then pinned it to his leather vest. With that task accomplished, he buttoned his jacket.

As soon as the rangers were out of sight, Chip hustled to the barn to get the buggy ready for Connie. He realized that his "plate" was going to be full for the next few days. He dearly hoped that he could keep up with all the chores.

One bright note: he didn't have to help with the stagecoach duties. His boss had arranged for Dusty Rhodes to assist Robert with that chore. For that he was most thankful.

Chapter Five

After many hours, and saddle-sore miles, the rangers completed the first leg of their journey.

"There's Payson—dead ahead," Jim reported.

"What time have ya got, Cap'?" Geoff asked.

"Almost three o'clock."

"We've made darn good time," Clint said.

"Indeed," Jim replied. "Let's stop at the livery first and get our horses tended to. We'll pay Marshal Chandler a quick visit after that."

"When do we eat?" Geoff wanted to know.

"After we check in at the hotel. I made our reservations before we left here yesterday," Jim said.

"Well, that was smart," acknowledged Dave.

"That's why they pay me the *big* bucks," Jim fired back, grinning.

After dropping the horses off at the livery, the rangers made their way to the town marshal's office. Marshal Mike Chandler was on station, patiently awaiting their arrival.

"Greetings, rangers," Mike said as the lawmen entered his office. "Have a seat. Make yerselves right at home."

For the next thirty minutes, Captain O'Bryan provided Mike with the details of the upcoming campaign. Mike rarely interrupted with a question. He mostly nodded his head as each element was brought to light.

"We're gonna head on over to the Cedar Grove Hotel and secure our rooms, Mike," Jim began, "and we'd like for you to join us for supper at the Yellow Sun Café—say in twenty minutes or so."

"Can do. I'll see ya there."

"Your deputy is also invited," Jim added.

"Kip is off today. I told 'im to rest up—'cause this place is all his for the next few days."

"I can relate to that!" Clint exclaimed. "I left my place in the hands of a young man, too."

At the hotel, the rangers found their rooms ready and waiting for them. Jim and Clint would share a room; Geoff, Dave and Titus would share another room. As soon as they finished stowing their gear in its proper place, they headed for the café.

Marshal Chandler was already seated at the back of the room at a long table. He waved his hand high in the air to get their attention. They spotted him right away. He was already sipping on a cup of black coffee.

As soon as they were all seated, an attractive young waitress arrived at the table. "What can I get y'all to drink?" she asked as her flirtatious blue eyes locked onto Dave Martin. She smiled at him.

Her flirting did not go unnoticed. Dave's brown eyes brightened considerably. He winked at her.

Everyone ordered coffee. "I'll be right back with your drinks," she said, her eyes still focused on Dave.

"What's her name, Mike?" Dave eagerly asked.

"Sarah Benson. She's nineteen. Been workin' here for 'bout two months," Mike replied.

"Hmmm, I don't recall seein' her two days ago when I was in here," Dave responded. "An' I shore wouldn't forget a face as lovely as hers."

"She might have been off duty that day," Mike supposed. "She's off at least two days each week."

In quick fashion, Sarah returned with their coffee. Next, she took their meal orders. While they were waiting for the food to arrive, the conversation again focused on the trip to Four Peaks. It soon came to light that, on several occasions, Marshal Chandler had traveled the route that they would soon embark upon. He knew precisely where the Sycamore Creek/Sugar Loaf Mountain rendezvous point was located.

"Just so ya know, Jim," Mike began, "I'll be bringin' along an additional packhorse. My rented packhorse will be carryin' two medium-sized tents and two five-gallon water bags.

"Also, I'll have some feed for our mounts. I'm guessin' that four twenty-pound bags of oats ought to be enough for the trip down and for one or two days that we are there. We can purchase more feed in Mesa City for our trip home. I was told that the governor is payin' our tab."

"Mesa City? Where's that, Mike?" Clint asked.

"It's not far from Sugar Loaf Mountain—perhaps a few miles to the southwest, and just a stone's throw from the Rio Salado. It was established in 1878—if my memory serves me right. It's pretty much a Mormon settlement. They named it Mesa City 'cause it sits atop a low plateau. There are probably fifteen hundred people livin' there— maybe more."

"Sounds like an interestin' place," Clint replied.

"The railroad builders must think so. They ran a line up there last year," added Mike.

"Anything else, Mike?" Clint asked.

"They got a newspaper—the *Mesa Free Press.*"

"Well, that's certainly an indication of growth," Clint commented. "Tell me more, Mike."

"They got these big ol' irrigation canals runnin' all over the place," continued Mike. "Most of 'em were built by the Hohokam Indians."

"The *Ho-ho* who?" Titus blurted out.

"Hohokam. Loosely translated, it means the 'Departed Ones'—or so I'm told. They have a long history in these parts that goes back five hundred or more years. I'd love to hear the whole story about 'em some day," Mike finally concluded.

Sarah returned with a helper and began placing the food on the table. Before walking away, she looked directly at Dave. "Is there anything else I can get for y'all?" she asked.

"I think, this will be all, Sarah," Mike said. "Thank you."

"I could handle some more coffee," Jim replied.

"Yeah, so could I," Geoff added.

After the coffee cups were refilled, Clint cleared his throat in preparation of telling everyone a story. He hoped it would be an interesting story.

"I hope y'all will bear with me, because I've just got to tell you a story," Clint said. "It's so ironic."

"Fire away," Jim said.

Clint leaned forward in his chair.

"When I first came to Arizona in the spring of '92, I was ridin' along the George Crook Trail and came to this wide spot between the ponderosa pines. To my left, it looked as though the earth just fell away. So I rode ol' Liberty in that direction. As y'all know—for you've seen it for yourselves—I was atop this great escarpment that ran east and west for miles and miles. Of course, I know it now as the Mogollon Rim.

"Anyway, it was all new to me then. I was speechless. I could see for seventy or eighty miles to the south out over the sprawlin' Tonto Basin. The one thing that caught my eye more than anything else was this really tall cluster of mountain peaks to the south. With the aid of my spyglass, I was able to count *four peaks* in close proximity to each other."

"I didn't know you could count that high, Clint," interrupted Jim, with a big grin forming on his face.

"Go sit on a prickly pear cactus, Jim," Clint fired back, grinning.

Laughter erupted around the table.

"Like I was sayin'," Clint continued, "this cluster of peaks haunted me all day. So, right then and there, I made a promise to myself that *one day* I would investigate those peaks. It was several months later when I learned from a friend that those peaks I saw were called Four Peaks.

"Now, here we are, about to embark on a trip to those very peaks. How *ironic* is that?" Clint asked, finishing his story.

"I'll bet this isn't the way ya envisioned payin' a visit to those peaks," Dave commented.

"No, it certainly isn't," agreed Clint. "But I have to admit, I'm glad that I will finally get to see 'em up close and personal."

"Well, I don't think them Kantrell boys will take kindly

to ya comin' down to visit their little mountain hideaway," added Dave, with a very serious look on his face.

"No, they certainly won't," agreed Clint.

Several minutes passed as other stories were shared.

From across the room, Sarah noticed that the lawmen were finishing up their meals. She hastily returned to their table one final time. "Will that be all, gentlemen?" she asked, while staring at Dave.

Mike nodded.

She placed the check in front of Mike, smiled at Dave, and walked away—taking with her some of the empty plates.

Clint looked down at his dinner plate, which was now almost void of food. It had been a delicious meal, but he preferred Connie's cooking more.

"I have got to say 'hello' to Betsy Lovemore before we leave here. I wonder if she will remember me? It's been a while since I was last in here."

"I'm sure she will, Clint," Jim said.

"Well, she oughta remember ya—seein' how ya are the dude that named this place," spouted Geoff.

"You heard that story, huh?" Clint said as he wiped his mouth with his napkin. "Yeah, I reckon I can take credit for that."

As they were paying their bill, Betsy Lovemore walked out of the kitchen. Clint got her attention and introduced himself. She remembered him and gave him a big hug.

"Long time, no see," she said. "Where the heck have you been, Ranger Wells?"

He briefly told her about his horse ranch to the east. He also mentioned his wife, Connie, and his little girl,

Lena. He did not, however, disclose the reason for his being in town.

Realizing that his friends had gone outside, Clint hastily finished up his chat with Betsy and excused himself.

"Reckon I'd best be goin'. My friends are waitin' for me outside. It was great seein' you again."

"It's so good to see you, too, Ranger Wells. I wish we had more time to visit."

"Yeah, me too," Clint replied as he gave her a goodbye hug.

"You come back ... and bring that wife and child of yours so I can meet them."

"I'll be sure to do that, ma'am," Clint promised as he reached for the door handle.

Clint joined his friends on the boardwalk. They had come outside rather than stand with Clint during his conversation with Mrs. Lovemore.

The sun had already set, and the air temperature was quickly falling. Clint's jacket was in his hotel room.

"Thanks for waitin' on me," Clint said.

"No problem," Jim replied.

"Mike, when does the café close?" Dave asked.

"Seven o'clock—normally. But I've never seen Betsy or her workers leave before seven-thirty. They gotta clean up the place, ya know," Mike answered.

"What's next, Cap'?" Geoff asked.

"It's almost six-thirty, so I suggest we mosey on over to the livery and check on our horses and tack. After that, we can head for the hotel," Jim said. "Tonight will be the last time we'll get to sleep in a good, comfortable bed for awhile."

"Oh, Captain, I plumb forgot about this here telegraph

message from Flag'," Mike said as he reached into his shirt pocket and produced a small sealed envelope.

Jim pealed the flap back and extracted the message. He mumbled every word to himself as he read each line. "Hallelujah!" he shouted as he read the last sentence and folded up the message.

"Important message, boss?" Dave inquired.

"Clint will certainly think so. It's from our boss, Major Williamson. Seems that Clint has been promoted by the headship in Phoenix to the rank of captain."

"What did you say?" asked Clint, looking a bit pale. "I've been promoted?"

"Here's the message, Clint. Read it for yourself."

Clint took the message from Jim and read it, not once, but twice. "I just don't believe it."

"Congratulations, Clint," Jim said as he extended his hand to his friend. "Couldn't have happened to a nicer feller."

The other lawmen joined in with their sincere congratulations as well.

"Ya definitely earned it, Clint," Mike replied as he slapped Clint on the back. "And I sincerely mean that."

"Thanks, fellers," Clint finally managed to say after shaking each extended hand.

"Rangers, this is where we split up. I'll see ya in the mornin'," Mike said as he turned and walked back to his office. He would be sleeping overnight at the jail. However, he still had rounds to make before calling it a day.

The rangers walked to the livery. Clint, especially, was concerned for his steed, Apache. This was the colt's first night away from the ranch, and he didn't know how the three-year-old would handle it.

Clint approached Jake, the stable master. "How's that big black been behavin' so far?" Clint asked.

"Well, so far, so good. He was uh snortin' and uh stompin' for a while, but soon settled in," Jake reported.

"Jake, if you have any problems with him, I'm stayin' in room *five* at the Cedar Grove Hotel. Don't hesitate to call on me," Clint instructed.

"Yes, sir, I'll shore do that."

"Does anyone spend the night here?" Jim asked as he scanned the inside of the barn.

"I'm here *every* night. Got myself a nice little room just over yonder," Jake replied as he pointed to a closed door some twenty feet away.

"That's certainly handy," commented Geoff.

"We'll be leavin' town 'round eight o'clock," Jim began, "so look for us to be here before then."

"I'll be up and ready for ya," Jake said. "I'll have 'em watered and fed by the time y'all arrive."

Jim nodded. "Thanks, Jake."

The rangers walked back to the hotel. Clint was feeling relieved that his colt was doing so well. The last thing he wanted was for the animal to get upset and injure himself trying to bust loose from his stall.

As the rangers got nearer to the hotel, they spotted Marshal Chandler just ahead of them. He was finishing up his rounds. They elected not to disturb him.

"If all the rangers are git'n fired in January, I gotta start scoutin' for a new job. I wonder if Mike could use another deputy?" Dave pondered aloud. "I think he would be a fair man to work for."

"And I'm not?" Jim asked.

"Oh, I didn't mean it like *that*, Captain!"

"I know you didn't. I'm just jerkin' your rein," Jim fired back, grinning.

"I *knew* that all along," Dave fibbed.

"You could ask him in the mornin' over coffee," Clint suggested. "I'm sure he could use a man with your experience. However, this town may not be able to afford your expert services."

"Yeah, that's how it can be sometimes. These little communities have a pretty tight budget," Jim added. "So, don't expect too much."

"I'd love to know just how much they is uh payin' that new *greenhorn* deputy that Mike just hired," Dave said, while scratching at the stubble on his face.

When the rangers entered the hotel, they espied the elderly desk clerk sitting in a chair behind the counter. He appeared to be asleep. Geoff faked a loud cough. It got results. The clerk sprang to his feet and greeted the rangers as they walked across the lobby to the staircase.

"Geoff, ya go on ahead to our room with Titus. I'll be up in a bit," Dave said.

Clint looked at Jim, who looked at Geoff, who looked at Titus. It was obvious that Dave had plans, and they didn't include sleep. Jim felt like he had to inflict his command position upon Dave to prevent any problems. He called the young ranger aside.

"Son, I know what you're up to, and it's fine with me if you want to return to the café and get better acquainted with that pretty waitress. But, I must insist that you be in your bed by ten o'clock … and that's an order," Jim said with firmness.

"I promise, Captain," Dave said as he nodded and looked his boss straight in the eye.

"Remember, you're an Arizona Ranger, so behave like

one. We don't need the badge tarnished by misbehavior. You *savvy*?"

"I'll be on my best behavior, Captain."

The rangers, except Dave, ascended the stairway to their rooms. Tomorrow would be an even longer day in the saddle, and everyone needed as much rest as possible—and that included Dave. Jim hoped he would obey orders and be in his room by ten. He thought about waiting up for Dave, but he was just too tired.

"What time is it, Cap'," Geoff asked.

Jim retrieved his gold pocket watch from his vest. "Almost seven-thirty."

"Hmmm, it's a bit too early to turn in," Geoff said. "I think, I'll go back downstairs and shoot some pool. I saw a pool table in that room next to the lobby. I love the game. Titus, ya wanna join me?"

"I'm game. The noise of the pool balls breakin' oughta keep that clerk awake," Titus said with a chuckle. "Or maybe not."

Jim nodded his approval. "That's fine with me, boys," he said, easily relenting to Geoff's passion. "You younger folks seem to function well on less sleep. Reckon I did, too, a very long time ago."

"Thanks, Cap'," Geoff said.

"Just don't disturb the hotel's other guest. We don't need any complaints directed at us," Jim concluded.

"Not a problem, sir," Geoff said. "Let's go, Titus!"

"Oh, by the way, the same curfew goes for the two of you, as well. I want you both in your beds by ten o'clock. Do you hear me?"

"Yes, sir! Loud and clear!" Geoff blurted out.

Clint and Jim went to their room. Once inside, Jim wasted no time in selecting a bed. He was asleep in ten short minutes. Clint, on the other hand, was not able to sleep. He had a lot on his mind.

There was a door in the room leading out onto a balcony. Clint elected to sit outside for a few minutes. He slipped on his denim jacket as he crossed the room in the direction of the door. Once outside, he could easily see the entire length of the main street, which was illuminated by several lampposts.

Two chairs were available on the balcony. He selected the closest one. It wasn't very comfortable. The night air had a slight chill, but not enough to make it too uncomfortable.

From the balcony, he could see the Yellow Sun Café, which was about fifty yards away. Under the faint glow of the lamppost, he could see Dave and Sarah talking. She was evidently getting off work. A minute later, they walked off together and disappeared into the darkness at the far end of the street.

He's probably walkin' her home, Clint thought.

Ninety minutes later, Clint retreated to the warmth of the room. He looked down at the empty bed before him and immediately thought about his own bed at the ranch. Last night, that bed had been adorned with his beautiful wife—this bed was cold and empty. Already, he deeply missed her presence.

Clint heard voices in the hallway. He went to the door and peeked out. It was Geoff and Titus. They were headed for their room. Clint glanced at his pocket watch. It was a quarter past nine. He was thankful that they had obeyed Jim's curfew order.

* * * * *

Dave and Sarah were sitting on a tree stump not far from her home. They had been sitting there for over an hour. The conversation had been light-hearted for the most part, but turned more serious with time.

Sarah was now sharing her life's story with a man she had become most infatuated with. It helped that he was glued to her every word. She felt like he really cared about her—a feeling that she had never truly experienced with a man before. Her scant nineteen years of life had been filled mostly with misery and loneliness. Poverty had been a big part of her life's experience, as well.

"I reckon I had best be git'n ya home, Sarah, before someone comes lookin' for ya," Dave suggested.

"I doubt that anyone would be too worried. In case you haven't noticed, Mr. Martin, I *am* a grown woman."

"Yes, ma'am, ya certainly are that. And, I might add, a very pretty woman, too."

"You *really* think so?" she said as her facial expression brightened considerably.

Before he could answer, she leaned over and kissed him squarely on the lips. She had never kissed a man before, and she surprised herself at how bold she was to do such a thing now.

Dave, for his part, enjoyed her boldness, and kissed her back, not once, but several times. He suddenly realized that he had found a girl that he could truly love.

* * * * *

Clint was awakened by footsteps in the hallway. He was a light sleeper, mainly due to having a child in his home. The slightest whimper from Lena would always arouse him from his slumber.

Quietly, he slipped out of his lumpy, rented bed and headed straight for the door. He eased the door open slightly and peeked out into the dimly lit hallway. It was Dave.

Satisfied, he returned to his bed and reached for his pocket watch that was lying on the bedside table. The light in the room was faint at best, but he could still see the Roman numerals. It was a few minutes past ten o'clock.

Close enough, he thought as he lay back down.

Clint's mind traveled back to the time when he was a young ranger in Texas and how lonely he was then. He felt sorry for Dave. It was his feeling that a young man like Dave should have a wife and family of his own by age twenty-seven.

Running all over the territory chasing outlaws is not a suitable life for a young man but, I guess someone has got to do it, Clint told himself.

Clint wondered if Dave had made arrangements to see the pretty young waitress again. If so, and things worked themselves out, he supposed that Dave might want to live and work in Payson after the rangers disbanded. He was already displaying a strong penchant to do just that.

Perhaps she will be working at the café in the morning … and Dave can see her one more time before we leave town. May it be the Lord's will, he inwardly prayed.

Clint fell asleep with that happy thought in the back of his mind.

* * * * *

Chip Bowman undressed and slipped into bed. He hurriedly pulled the two heavy blankets over his body and then, all the way up to his chin. He was feeling the late evening chill in the room. He had elected not to light a fire in the woodstove. He would save the wood for when he really needed it.

His first day without the assistance of his boss had gone well. All the required chores were done, and almost in the usual allotted time. Nonetheless, before retiring to his room, he had carefully gone over everything in his mind to ensure that he hadn't forgotten something. Nothing came to mind.

Mrs. Wells said that her brother might come by and help me when he had time. That's fine with me, Chip muttered aloud.

Moments later, the tired and sore wrangler was fast asleep.

* * * * *

Connie Wells lay in her bed staring at the ceiling. The big bed seemed even bigger without her man lying next to her. She didn't like the feeling.

She thought back over the prior night when her husband was in this room with her. It had felt good having his strong arms wrapped snuggly about her yielding body.

I can't believe that I woke him at one o'clock in the morning for more lovemaking, she thought quietly to herself. *He must think I'm a terrible strumpet?*

Connie chuckled inaudibly at the very thought. She knew full well that her husband didn't think *that*, not even for a second. In fact, she rightly supposed that he had enjoyed every minute of their early morning lovemaking.

Deep in her brain, she slowly and calculatingly began to replay the gratifying experience that took place in their bed so early in the morning. Several minutes passed before she became aware that her sexual thoughts were causing her breathing to gradually accelerate. Then, when her heart started pounding, she knew it was time to apply the brakes to her brain.

Whoa! Connie inwardly shouted to her brain. *Please, focus on something else.*

Connie climbed out of bed, washed her face in cool water, and went into the other bedroom to check on Lena before returning to bed.

Later, with some effort, Connie was soon sleeping soundly.

Chapter Six

Friday, October 9th.

Dave Martin got to see Sarah Benson one more time—
over breakfast at the Yellow Sun Café. It was very obvious to Clint and the other lawmen that the ranger and
the waitress had special feelings for each other. All were
happy for them.

The rangers, along with Marshal Chandler, rode out
of Payson shortly before eight o'clock. They had a rather
long day of riding ahead of them. It was slightly more
than fifty miles to the rendezvous point, and they hoped
to cover half that distance by late afternoon. Sunset this
time of year was around six o'clock, and they wanted ample time to set up a proper campsite before day's end.

Normally, riding twenty-five miles in one day was no
big deal, but not in this case, for the terrain was chal-
lenging. They would be facing steep grades at several
points along the route. With packhorses in-tow, the ride
would be slow and tiring. And, later in the day, they
would have to contend with the desert heat. Mike, who

was leading the group, planned to stop three or four times to rest the horses.

As they moved south, Mike also took on the job of tour guide. He was very knowledgeable of the route. On a number of occasions, he directed their attention to several points of interest. He was even able to identify the many different types of plants and trees. In short, he made the trip very educational.

"I got to say, Mike, you certainly know a lot about this here country," Jim commented.

"Oh, I had a pretty good teacher—an old prospector by the name of Ken Jaynes. I traveled this route with 'im a couple of years ago. He claimed to have a gold mine with a good supply of dust over in them mysterious Superstition Mountains."

"Where are these Superstition Mountains?" Clint asked as he scanned the vistas about him.

"Not far from Four Peaks. Just a bit to the southeast," Mike replied. "Can't see 'em from here."

"How soon before we see ol' Four Peaks from this road we is now travelin'?" Geoff asked.

"Oh, probably by mid-day tomorrow," Mike replied.

"What else will we see today?" Titus asked.

"Hmmm, let me think," Mike said as he scratched his unshaven cheek. "We've already seen North Peak, so I reckon we'll be seein' Mazatzal Peak. It's a bit higher in elevation than Four Peaks—though not by a whole lot."

"Anything else?" Titus asked.

Mike rubbed at his cheek a second time. "I can't recall off hand. There's Mount Ord, but I don't think we'll see it until tomorrow."

"I think I'd like to see them ol' Superstition Mountains some day—up close and personal," Clint said.

"Ya are likely as not to get yer head shot off if ya come too close. Them cagey ol' miners are a strange bunch. Rather loony—if ya ask me. They don't cotton much to outsiders snoopin' around *their* mountain," Mike cautioned.

"Are you bein' serious?" Jim asked.

"Yep, as serious as a man can be. Many a stranger has wandered into them mountains and not come back. My guess is that they probably ended up as buzzard bait," Mike concluded.

"Maybe I won't go there after all," Clint said.

The farther south they rode, the more elevation they gave up. From Payson (elevation 4,930') to Sugar Loaf Mountain there was a gradual drop of approximately three thousand feet in elevation. And with each thousand feet, the ambient air temperature was rising by as much as three to four degrees.

The landscape was steadily changing, too. Cedar and a few junipers had now replaced the ponderosa pines. And, there were more chaparral-like plants, along with a good helping of prickly pear. The soil had become sandier and was heavily littered with stones. The once abundant grassy areas were gradually disappearing.

Clint was the first to comment on their surroundings. "Mike, it looks like we're git'n into a more desert-like environment. I already miss the big ponderosa pines."

"Yeah, me too," Mike readily agreed. "Nothin' more ugly than mesquite or creosote bush."

"Oh, I don't know," Clint began, "they don't look so bad to me. Reminds me of the vegetation in the Big Bend country."

"Clint, have ya ever seen a big Saguaro?" Mike asked.

"Can't say that I have—not even in a picture. But, I've heard of 'em."

"Now that's *real* beauty! I was in total awe the first time I saw one. They can get pretty darn tall. I hear they can live for three hundred years or more," Mike began, "and they don't sprout their first arm until they're nearly a hundred years old."

"When will we see one?" Clint asked.

"Tomorrow—for shore," Mike answered.

"Mike, I think you missed your callin'," Clint commented. "You should have been a tour guide for the stage line. Those bug-eyed Easterners are always starvin' for information on the West."

"I don't think that would work out so well for me," Mike quickly declared, "'cause I ain't got much use for a *tenderfoot*."

By mid-day the rangers stopped for the second time. They were now about fourteen miles south of Payson. Unlike their first stop—a shady ravine along the side of the road—they were now at a way station that was located about five hundred yards west of the main road. This stop would be much longer to allow time for everyone to eat lunch. Also, there was a fresh-water well here, and the horses would be able to get a proper drink from the big, round, metal storage tank.

The station manager greeted them on arrival. "Welcome to Rye Creek Station. Ya headin' north or south?"

"South," Mike responded.

"This is a nice place," Clint said to the manager as he tied his horse to the hitching rail. "This box canyon provides a natural oasis for this way station. Except for the road we rode in on, the only way out of here is straight up those canyon walls."

"Yeah, it's certainly well protected from the hot desert winds and dust storms," the manager said.

"I see," said Clint.

"Y'all help yerselves to the water. Let me know if ya need anything else," the manager concluded as he walked back into the station house.

"I'm famished!" declared Geoff. "Let's eat!"

"Whoa, partner! You and the others get them horses watered before you break out the box lunches," Jim ordered. "And give 'em some feed, too."

In Geoff's defense, Betsy and Sarah had prepared box lunches for the lawmen earlier that morning, and Geoff was more than eager to devour his. He knew the roast beef sandwiches and side dishes would be delicious.

Betsy, feeling that it was her civic duty to help the lawmen, provided the lunches—free of charge. She claimed that providing at least one quality meal for them was the least she could do to support the lawmen in their effort to rid the territory of criminals.

"We shore could use a cool breeze. It's uh git'n a lot warmer 'round here," Titus said as he dabbed sweat from his brow with his bandana.

"You got that right," agreed Clint.

"Deal with it, rangers," Mike began, "'cause it's gonna get even warmer than this. It can still reach *ninety* degrees in the desert in early October."

"Ninety!" Titus exclaimed. "Ya can have it. I think I'll stick to the higher elevations."

"Be shore to top off the water bags and fill yer canteens," Mike said, "'cause it's a good ways to the next way station."

"How far is it?" asked Jim.

"Another ten *hard* miles—or more," Mike replied with

a slight sigh. "We'll make another stop between here and the next way station to rest the horses. The next station will mark the half-way point of our journey to Sugar Loaf."

"That's good," Dave said, "'cause I'm ready to quit now."

"As for our next stop—keep yer eyes peeled for a cluster of cottonwood trees. They usually pop up around watering holes and creeks," Mike instructed the rangers. "If we don't find any water near 'em—we'll at least have some shade from the sun."

The rangers rested at Rye Creek for nearly an hour before bidding their gracious host farewell, mounting up, and riding southwest again. The sun was high overhead, and the air was dry and getting a bit too warm for their liking.

"I hear the nighttime temperature in the Sonoran desert can vary by as much as thirty degrees from the daytime temperature," Clint commented.

"That's a fact, Clint," Mike confirmed. "And it's especially true in the winter months when the temperature drops rather quickly after sunset."

"I'm glad I included a heavy wool blanket with my bedroll," Clint replied. "Sounds like I'm gonna need it durin' the night."

It was three o'clock when the lawmen stopped under a row of cottonwoods for a breather. They were roughly twenty miles south of Payson. After a forty-five minute break, they mounted up and continued their southwest trek.

"Sorry, Jim, that that ol' creek bed turned out to be a

dry hole," Mike said. "It hasn't rained in a good while ... and them ol' cottonwoods can soak up what little moisture is available."

"Not a problem. We've still got an ample supply of water in our water bags. We'll ride another hour—maybe two—and call it a day," Jim said. "I hope we reach that next way station by then."

"Sounds like a plan to me," Clint responded as he patted Apache on the neck. He was pleased at how well his steed was holding up. It reminded him of how well his stallion, Liberty, had done on so many of these outings in days gone by.

Shortly before five o'clock, Jim called a halt to the forward progress. "This is as far as we go today," he began, "if'n we want to get a proper campsite set up before dark. Besides that ... I'm dog-tired."

"I wonder where that next way station is?" Titus said.

"Probably not more'n a mile or two up the road," Mike guessed. "But, like Jim, I'm exhausted ... and ready to stop for a good, long spell."

"This certainly looks like a good place to set up a campsite," Clint said as he looked around.

"Looks good to me," Dave said.

"Y'all know the routine," Jim said as he dismounted. "Let's get our 'tent city' set up and start some grub uh cookin' on the ol' campfire."

The lawmen quickly busied themselves with the unloading of the packhorses. Once their campsite was set up, they unsaddled their horses and tended to their needs. Each horse was given an ample helping of oats. Clint filled his hat with water from one of the water bags and held it out for his horse, Apache, to drink from. The young colt drank readily from the hat. After three hatfuls, Clint cut him off so that the other horses could drink their share.

"I wish we were near that creek you spoke of," Clint said, directing his comment toward Mike. "This horse of mine could use a lot more water."

"We'll run across Sycamore Creek tomorrow," Mike assured his friend.

"Go figure—we don't even have two sturdy trees 'round here to set up a proper picket line for our horses," Geoff complained. "Now what?"

"We'll have to hobble 'em," Jim said. "And we'll stand guard duty tonight. We can't have someone sneakin' in here and stealin' our mounts."

The sun was setting by the time the campsite was fully operational. Dinner was heating up over the campfire. The tents were up, the bedrolls were all laid out, and the tarps were in place above the tents.

"Anyone got a guitar? We can sing a few fireside songs," Dave said, and then he started to laugh.

"Did ya sing for that little gal at the café?" Geoff wanted to know. (He frequently teased his friend.)

"None of yer dang business!" Dave fired back, showing a bit of ire.

"Now, now, let's not get our feathers ruffled," said Jim, intervening before things got out of hand. "You oughta know, Geoff, that a man's love interest is his own business."

"Aw, I was just teasin' 'im, Cap'. I don't mean no harm," Geoff explained. "Sorry, Dave. I'll let it be."

"That's okay," Dave responded, while kicking his boot

in the dust. "I reckon I'm a bit too touchy 'bout that girl. She's real nice, and I like her a lot. I just wanna make it through this upcomin' campaign so I can git back to her."

"Now, Dave, don't ya be worrin' yerself 'bout git'n out of this deal in one piece. We is *all* gonna git home safe and sound," Geoff declared without any hesitation. "I *guarantee* it!"

Clint felt it was wrong for Geoff to make such a bold claim, even if his intentions were good.

"It's my sincere belief ..."

Clint stopped mid-sentence. He had come close to refuting Geoff's comment to Dave, but changed his mind. In his own understanding, Clint knew that God's will always trumps men's desires. Fact is, no matter how careful they might be, it was for God to decide if they *all* would return home safely.

"That's right, Dave," Jim added. "We've always watched each other's back. And, best of all, we've got a lot of nice folks prayin' for us."

"Was ya about to say somethin', Clint?" Geoff asked.

"Naw, I must have been thinkin' out loud."

For the next several minutes no one spoke much. Perhaps they were preoccupied with thoughts of their future.

After dinner, the cookware was cleaned and the horses were checked on. The lawmen discussed the order in which the guard duty would be assigned. Dave would take the first watch. Clint ended up with the final watch. He was glad about that. It meant he could sleep longer without being disturbed.

"It's likely I don't need to remind y'all—but I will just

the same—to be alert for critters," Mike cautioned. "Them ol' scorpions are thick 'round here. Check yer bedroll before ya crawl in it. And, come mornin'—shake out yer boots real good before ya stick yer doggies in 'em.

"And, one last item to keep in mind," Mike continued, "the rattlesnakes like to prowl the desert at night—so watch where ya walk."

"That's it! I'm headin' back to Payson!" Dave exclaimed. (It was hard to tell if he was kidding or not.) "This desert sounds more dangerous than Kantrell and his cutthroats."

"Shore sounds like it to me, too!" Geoff grumbled in agreement.

"Wait until ya hear them coyotes uh howlin' in the middle of the night. I've had 'em run right smack through my campsite," Mike added to his other warnings.

"How many hours until daylight, Captain?" Dave asked. "Reckon I'm gonna be a nervous wreck until then."

Everyone laughed.

"Well, I don't know about the rest of you, but I'm turnin' in for the night," Clint said. He was feeling the results of the day's ride. His lower back was hurting him the most. It had been quite some time since he last spent that many hours in the saddle.

"Goodnight, Clint," Jim said.

The others echoed Jim's words as they made their way to their own bedroll.

"Same to y'all," Clint said.

Dave, who had the first watch, grabbed his carbine and positioned himself atop a large boulder not far from the campfire. He carefully looked around his perch for snakes and scorpions before he got comfortable.

He spent most of his guard duty thinking about Sarah. He was hopelessly in love with her. He murmured a silent prayer for himself *and* her—that one day they would be reunited once again. His mind raced over the events of the previous night. How wonderful her kisses had been.

As for Clint, he lay awake in his bedroll for a long spell before falling asleep. His mind was once again on his family. He missed them more than he could possibly express. He prayed that the upcoming raid on Kantrell's hideout would not result in the death of any of his friends—or his own death for that matter.

It's not God's will that I should worry, he thought. *It's out of my hands.*

Jim lay awake for several minutes, as well. He prayed that God would give him the wisdom that was needed before he led his men into battle. This was his first big campaign as a leader. In the past, Major Williamson had had that dubious honor. Now the responsibility was his and his alone.

Jim knew he could always count on God for answers.

I know I can count on Clint, too, to keep me focused, he thought. *It's no fluke that he got promoted to captain. Clint is as sharp as they come.*

Geoff's mind was on the upcoming demise of the rangers. *How can the governor put us out to pasture? And just like that, without even a pat on the back*, he thought. Suddenly, he felt unappreciated and neglected by his governmental leaders.

Titus sat outside the tent he shared with Geoff. He wanted one last smoke before retiring to his bedroll. He lit up a half-smoked, store-bought cheroot that he had been nursing most of the day. He enjoyed the taste of a cheroot much more than a normally rolled cigarette.

Tomorrow would bring him and the others closer to danger, and his mind was turning over and over something that Clint had said a couple of days ago: *I don't put much faith in luck.*

It was undeniably obvious to Titus that Clint was a believer in God and Jesus and prayer. He knew that Clint even carried a small Bible with him. And, he had even seen him reading it the other morning. For whatever reason, it seemed that Titus' faith in some unseen god did not make a lot of sense to him.

I just don't understand how anyone can believe all that Bible stuff, he thought as he finished his cheroot. *Perhaps, one of these days, I'll ask Clint to explain his Christian faith to me.*

Titus attempted to ease his way into the tent so as not to disturb Geoff.

"I was wonderin' if ya were ever gonna turn in," Geoff whispered.

"Sorry, Geoff. Did I wake ya?" Titus asked in a low voice.

"Naw, I couldn't sleep. Too much stuff floatin' 'round in my head."

"Yeah, mine too," confessed Titus. "Geoff, can I ask ya somethin'?"

"I reckon."

"Do ya believe in *luck?*"

"I never gave it much thought. I confess that I use that *word* all the time," Geoff began, "but I sorta like to think that I have a *guardian angel* watchin' over me. It makes me feel safer."

Geoff let out a big yawn and rubbed his eyes. "Maybe

ya should talk to Captain Wells," Geoff suggested. "He's good at explainin' things. He's always steered me in the right direction."

"I considered that," Titus confessed.

"Reckon we'd best be git'n some shuteye," Geoff concluded as he rolled over onto his side.

"Yeah, reckon so. Goodnight, Geoff."

"Goodnight to you, Titus."

Geoff and Titus were soon fast asleep.

Mike, on the other hand was still awake and feeling rather unsettled. He rolled from his left side onto his right side in an effort to get comfortable. It didn't work. He finally flipped over onto his back and placed his arms over his lower chest and locked his fingers together. *Maybe this will work*, he muttered quietly to himself.

Mike's biggest problem was not his lack of comfort, but that he could not stop worrying about the *greenhorn* deputy that he left in charge back in Payson. It was keeping him in a relatively tense frame of mind.

Got to let it go, he softly whispered.

Mike took in a deep breath and let it out slowly. He repeated this several times. It was working. His mind began to clear. In minutes he was asleep.

Tomorrow would be a day of gathering together at Sugar Loaf Mountain for all the lawmen involved in the campaign against Kantrell and his followers.

* * * * *

Twenty-seven miles south of Captain O'Bryan's camp, a group of five men were bedding down for the night at the base of Sugar Loaf Mountain. They had spent most of the afternoon erecting a large canvas tent. This tent would be the temporary headquarters for the largest anti-crime campaign ever undertaken in the history of the Arizona Territory.

One of the five individuals was a special envoy from the governor's office. It was his job to carry out the governor's mandate of eradicating the criminal populace. The governor did not hand out any specific guidelines—he just wanted results. His primary goal was to see Arizona achieve statehood one day, but he realized Washington would never approve it as long as large bands of outlaws were running amok all over the territory.

The envoy wasn't certain how many lawmen would show up on Saturday, but he hoped for at least fifty men. Based on recent reports that he had received, it would take that many lawmen to fight an evenly matched battle with the outlaws.

Before retiring, he had gone over his detailed map of the area. He was reasonably satisfied that he could get his lawmen to Wild Burro Canyon without being detected—for he had a hidden "ace-in-the-hole." This raid had been in the planning stages for two months, and special precautions had been taken. He would reveal his hidden "ace" when everyone was assembled for duty.

Tomorrow, would be Day One of a new beginning for the Arizona Territory. Hopefully, within a few days, Easterners would no longer look upon Arizona as an uncivilized land.

Presently, most Easterners were passing *through* Arizona on their way to California. Not many could be coaxed into settling down in the territory. Many travelers wrongly believed that the various Apache tribes were still on the warpath. It didn't seem to matter that it was well publicized that most of them were now peaceable and living on the San Carlos Reservation and several other reservations in the East.

Ruthless white men and Mexican bandits were now committing most of the killings in the territory. There were even civilized ranchers killing each other over animal grazing rights. It amounted to a war of sheep vs. cattle. Grazing land was at a premium in Arizona. The past few years of drought hadn't helped the situation either.

Must be them silly "dime novels" folks are reading that's scaring them off, he thought.

Chapter Seven

Saturday, October 10th.

Clint extracted his pocket watch from his vest pocket and checked the time. It was almost six o'clock. He decided to extend his guard duty another thirty minutes to allow his friends a little more time to sleep. To the east, he could see a faint glimmer of light. In another thirty or forty minutes the sun would break above the distant mountain range.

Clint walked over to the campfire and added another log. He was feeling a bit cold even though he was wearing his fleece-lined denim jacket and had a heavy, woolen blanket draped about his shoulders.

Brrr! Mike was right, the dry desert air can get mighty cold at night, Clint mumbled to himself as he laid aside the blanket in preparation of searching for more firewood.

After gathering more wood, and a few minutes prior to waking his slumbering friends, Clint prepared the coffee. He knew they would appreciate it a lot. When the sun finally peered over the ridge, Clint woke up his traveling companions. Now, as for being woke up—*that* they didn't appreciate.

"Out of them bedrolls! The sun is up and so should you be!" he hollered.

After several moans and groans and a few testy words, everyone rolled out to greet the new day.

"Hey, the coffee is already uh brewin'!" Geoff said as a gratifying smile formed on his face. "Thanks, Captain Wells! Ya are a good man."

"Not a problem, my friend," Clint said. "And, if you don't mind, go easy on that *captain* stuff. I rather feel like Jim is the only captain on this outing. We don't need any confusion."

"Sorry, Clint," Geoff said. "I just figured—"

"It's okay, Geoff," Clint interrupted. "Reckon I'm just a lot more comfortable with folks using my first name for a while longer. Perhaps one day ..."

Clint didn't finish his sentence.

Dave and Titus took note of Clint's preference.

It was approaching eight-thirty when the rangers and the marshal broke camp and rode out. Except for a small fire pit and a circle of stones surrounding it, they left behind no visible signs that they had utilized the area.

"Maybe we'll stop here again on our way back home," Mike said. "It was a right decent campsite."

"Yeah, and no nasty critters showed up to spoil it for us," Dave quickly added.

Twenty minutes into their ride, the lawmen arrived at the narrow road leading to the second way station that they were hoping to reach yesterday. They could even see the station from their present position. It was about a hundred yards to the east.

"Are we gonna pay 'em a visit?" Titus asked.

"Reckon not," Jim said. "We'll keep movin' south. I want to take advantage of this cool mornin' air. It benefits the horses."

The lawmen rode on until half past ten before taking their first break. Mike estimated that they were, more or less, thirty-five miles south of Payson. After a well-merited rest, they were back in the saddle and on the move again.

Another hour passed by the time the lawmen reined up on top of a low ridge. From this vantage point, they could see for many miles to the south. Mike carefully scouted the horizon to get his bearings.

"Are we git'n any closer to that ol' creek, Mike?" Jim wanted to know.

"Yes, sir," Mike replied. "I'd say we are almost on top of it. See that heavy growth of small trees and those few tall cottonwoods over yonder?"

"Yeah, I do. They look to be a mile or less away," Jim surmised.

"We'll go on down this road a short piece and then cut a path over that way," Mike instructed.

"What's that cloud of dust comin' straight for us?" asked Dave. "Is that one of 'em ol' *dust devils* I heard 'bout?"

"It's just a guess, but I'd say it's the Red Mountain Transit Company stagecoach," Mike replied. "We'd better wait here—just off the roadway—until it passes."

"The dust is blowin' to our left, so let's move to the far right-hand side of the road," Jim cautioned. "No sense git'n any dustier than we are already."

Six minutes later the stagecoach rumbled past

the lawmen. The driver and shot gunner smiled and waved. The lawmen returned the courtesy. They also allowed a minute or two more for the dust to settle before moving on.

Twenty minutes later, the lawmen reined up at the bank of Sycamore Creek. There wasn't a lot of water flowing in the creek at this location, but it looked clean and refreshing. Jim ordered everyone to dismount and water his horse.

Clint removed the red bandana from his neck, dipped it in the water, and washed his face and neck. It refreshed him. He dipped it in the water once more, rung it out, and then re-tied it around his neck. *That ought to keep me cool for a little while*, he thought.

"Mike, what's that structure over yonder?" asked Jim, pointing to an almost hidden building about one mile to the south of their present location.

"I believe that's another way station for the Red Mountain Transit Company."

"Reckon we could have gone there for water?" Jim surmised as he finished watering his horse.

"Yes, sir, we certainly could have. I didn't realize that we were this close to it. Sorry."

"That's okay. Don't worry about it," Jim said. "The water here is just fine."

"Jim, it's almost twenty till one," Clint said as he looked at his watch. "What do you say to spendin' some extra time here and havin' some lunch?"

"Sounds like a good plan to me, Cap'," declared Geoff. "I'm git'n plenty hungry."

"Yeah, I could eat a bite, too," Dave added.

"I'm certainly hungry," Mike said.

Titus was hungry, as well, but made no comment about his needs.

"We've got some shade here under these cottonwoods," Mike said as he glanced up at the overhanging branches. "It would be nice to get out of the sun for awhile."

"Okay, y'all won me over!" Jim exclaimed.

The lawmen soon had a temporary campsite set up. Titus gathered wood for the campfire. And, a short time later, they had some beans warming in a pot. Hard tack and beans didn't qualify as gourmet cooking by any means, but it filled a man's belly when he was starving.

An hour later, the lawmen were back in the saddle and riding south once more. Without a cloud in the sky to shield them, the sun would be beating down unmercifully on their bodies for the rest of the afternoon.

"It's git'n a lot warmer out here, Captain," Dave complained as he popped the cap on his canteen for a drink of cool water.

"That's for shore," Geoff quickly agreed as he pulled his hat down lower over his eyes.

Minutes later, they passed the road leading to the third way station. Again, Jim elected not to stop. There would be nothing to gain—only loss of time getting to their destination.

And, getting to Sugar Loaf Mountain was all that Clint could think of, too. He was still feeling the pain in his lower back. Apache had a smooth gait but, for the moment, it was of little consolation to him.

After riding a couple of more miles, they came to an area atop a high ridge filled with enormous boulders. Some were piled high on top of each other. To their left, some two hundred yards away, was a rock wall several hundred feet high. Below the wall was a deep ravine that cut a path south for a half-mile or more.

"Wow!" exclaimed Jim. "What a scenic spot."

"And look out there!" Clint shouted, pointing his finger. "I see a big ol' Saguaro!"

"Good eye, Clint," said Mike, confirming Clint's sighting. "And, before too long, we'll see thousands of 'em dot'n the landscape."

"I can hardly wait," Clint enthusiastically remarked.

After riding a few more miles, another new vista opened up to them.

"Look at that," Dave said. "The land is nearly as flat as a pancake as far as the eye can see."

"Over that way is Mesa City. And if ya look to yer left ya can see the top half of Four Peaks. It won't be much longer before ya will be able to see a lot more of the Peaks," Mike said.

Jim looked at his watch. It was three o'clock. "How far to Sugar Loaf, Mike?" Jim asked.

"Two hours—perhaps a bit less," he reported with some uncertainty. "I'm guessin' we're about eight miles away. But not more'n ten."

"Cap', do ya think most of 'em other lawmen are already at Sugar Loaf?" Geoff asked.

"I'm sure several have arrived ahead of us," Jim replied. "We'll find out soon enough."

Forty minutes later, Mike pointed out a new landmark. He directed everyone's attention to the left and out across the vast open expanse.

"There they are, Clint—the Superstition Mountains!" exclaimed Mike, pointing to the southeast. "And of course, we can see a lot more of Four Peaks from here."

"That ol' Superstition has a profile like no other mountain we've seen the past two days," Clint commented. "It looks like it's just one layer of rock stacked neatly on top of another."

"Yeah, I reckon it does look that way," agreed Mike. "That one section on the right that protrudes out near the top is called the Flat Iron. It's about four thousand feet above sea level."

"What's that tall, pointy rock to the left?" asked Clint, while peering through his telescoping spyglass. "It looks like a big, fat finger pointin' angrily up at the sky."

"That would be Weaver's Needle," Mike replied.

"Hmmm, quite interestin'," Clint replied.

Captain O'Bryan glanced at his pocket watch. It was nearly four o'clock. He was hoping to see Sugar Loaf Mountain by this late hour. He knew the horses were tired—as well as his men.

"Are we about there, yet?" Jim asked of Mike.

"One more hour at most, Captain," he responded with

a bit more certainty. "I'd say this is as good a place as any to take a quick break."

"I definitely agree," Jim said. "Dismount, men. Take fifteen."

After a brief rest, the lawmen mounted up and continued their trek south. They were all starting to get impatient as several more miles passed beneath their saddles.

Jim, his body aching somewhat, repeated his previous question. "Mike, are we about there, yet?"

"Well, sir," Mike began, "if ya look to yer right—say about a mile or two—ya can see the unmistakable shape of Sugar Loaf."

"Thank goodness!" exclaimed Jim, with a sigh.

Everyone immediately echoed the same sentiment. It had been a long day.

Thirty minutes later, the lawmen turned off the main road and headed down a narrow trail to the base of Sugar Loaf Mountain. A more substantial Sycamore Creek flowed nearby. Jim took out his pocket watch. It was a few minutes past five o'clock. They had roughly one hour of daylight left.

As they approached the rendezvous point, they espied a group of twenty or more men setting up several different campsites. A rather large tent had already been erected and was in the midst of the smaller tents.

"This must be it, men," Jim said. "Dismount and take care of your horses. I'll find out who's in charge of this camp and where they want us to set up our tents."

Five minutes later, Jim returned to his men. There was a tall, thin man walking at his side. He looked to be about fifty years old—judging by his graying hair.

"Men, this is Mr. Henry Watts. He's the governor's special envoy ... and he's been put in charge of this operation. We take our orders from him."

Each lawman extended his hand in greeting. Mr. Watts shook each hand and offered a hearty welcome. After the introductions were completed, Mr. Watts pointed to a location where the lawmen could set up their campsite. He then informed them that there would be a general meeting at the main tent at seven o'clock. He said he expected most of the participants to be on station by that hour.

It took about thirty minutes for Captain O'Bryan's team to get their packhorses unloaded and their mounts unsaddled. Their next task was to get the campsite set up, and they wasted no time in getting after it. The previous day's exercise in campsite preparation was paying off—this time, they displayed a lot more proficiency in getting the task done more smoothly.

"Practice makes us a bit more perfect, huh?" Jim commented as he looked around at his men.

"If ya say so, Captain," replied Dave, grinning.

As soon as they were done, Geoff roamed about the different campsites to count heads. He soon returned—with a disappointed look on his face.

"Cap'," Geoff began, "I counted twenty-eight able-bodied souls in this camp—including us and Mr. Watts. There are four other men, but I'm not includin' 'em in the count. They are only aides to Mr. Watts."

"I shore do hope a few more lawmen show up," Dave said as he glanced about the area.

"It would be nice," remarked Clint, with a sigh.

"There's still some daylight left," Jim reminded everyone. "I believe there will be a few more men ridin' in soon."

The words had hardly left his mouth when two more riders appeared on the low ridge above them. The new arrivals were not strangers to Dave and Geoff.

"Hey, Captain, look who's here!" Dave said with jubilation in his voice. "It's our ol' saddle pals, Chino and Dewey, from the Prescott office."

"Indeed, it is!" said Jim, smiling.

Chino Watson and Dewey Loomis spotted the rangers and rode over to them. They dismounted and greeted their fellow rangers. Dave quickly introduced them to Clint, Mike and Titus. Handshakes were cordially exchanged.

"Is this it?" Chino asked. "I don't see many badges roamin' about the place. I was hopin' there would be a *hundred* or more of us."

"This is it—so far," replied Geoff, with a sigh.

As the lawmen were talking, Mr. Watts walked up and introduced himself to the two new arrivals. They were, in due course, informed of the meeting. After a few brief words of gratitude for volunteering for special duty, Mr. Watts hastily returned to the main tent.

"We volunteered?" Chino said as he looked at Dewey with a stunned expression.

"Ha! That's news to me," grunted Dewey.

"I reckon it depends on what your *definition* of the word 'volunteer' is, huh?" quipped Jim.

Everyone laughed.

"Whether you're volunteers or not—we don't care. We're just delighted that you're here with us," declared Clint.

"Well, gents, ya just as well set up yer campsite with ours," Geoff said to Chino and Dewey. "Later we can sit about and chew the fat until that meetin' is called to order."

After Chino and Dewey finished setting up their campsite, they joined Jim and the others for meaningless conversation. It had been a long time since the rangers had all been in the same place at the same time—and there was a lot of news and story telling to catch up on.

While they were swapping yarns, three more riders topped the ridge. No one at Captain O'Bryan's campsite knew them. The three riders all looked very young—perhaps only in their late teens to middle twenties.

"Do ya know 'em, Captain?" Chino asked.

"Hmmm, can't say that I do," Jim replied with a slight hesitation.

"Jim, I *think* those are deputy sheriff badges they are wearin'," Clint said after closer inspection.

Jim nodded. "Yes, I believe you're right."

At that moment, Mr. Watts exited his tent, walked

part way up the road, and greeted the new arrivals. The three deputies quickly slid from their saddles and heartily returned the greeting. From all the repartee, it appeared that Mr. Watts was well acquainted with the three young deputies.

The new arrivals followed Mr. Watts back down the road. He immediately directed them to a spot where they could set up their own campsite.

A few minutes after the six o'clock hour, two more riders showed up. Mr. Watts, as was his custom, exited his tent and walked a short distance up the road to greet them, and ultimately show them where to establish their campsite.

Captain O'Bryan and his rangers, along with Marshal Chandler, talked on and on as darkness enveloped the area.

Clint checked his watch in the light of the campfire. "Jim, it's almost seven o'clock."

"Thanks, Clint," Jim replied. "Okay, men, let's mosey over to Watts' headquarters. That meetin' will be startin' at any moment. We don't want to make a bad impression by bein' late."

Captain O'Bryan began walking in the direction of the main tent with his entourage of lawmen following close behind.

* * * * *

This would be Connie's third night without Clint. She was sitting on the porch—with Lena perched on her lap—feeling a little blue. The only thing that prevented her from sliding into despair was her faith in God. She remembered what Jesus said: *Have faith in God* (Mark

11:22). She realized that there wasn't a thing she could do for her husband except pray for him and have faith that God would protect him.

Before departing the ranch, Clint had given his wife a basic overview of Captain O'Bryan's itinerary. She had been glad about that. According to the itinerary, the rangers would arrive at Sugar Loaf Mountain before sunset today. She wondered if they did, and how they were all doing. She was also concerned about Clint's three-year-old colt, Apache, and if he was performing well. She certainly hoped so.

Connie was glad that she had the mercantile store and café to keep her mind busy during the day and off of the concerns that troubled her. The store and café had been a busy place over the summer months, and she hoped both would continue to be busy during the winter months. It wouldn't be too long before she got her answer. Winter was virtually knocking at the door.

Connie realized, as did her aunt, that there would likely be days that the stage would not be able to get through due to the deep snows, and the same would be true for the supply wagons bringing new products to the store.

The sun was beginning to set, and Connie decided to take Lena inside. Besides, a chill was rapidly replacing the warmer air. As she rose from the rocking chair, she heard footsteps approaching. It was Chip Bowman.

"Hello, Chip," she said.

Lena smiled and waved her little hand. Chip quickly waved back.

"Howdy, Mrs. Wells. I just moseyed over to see if there was anything that I might be overlookin' before I called it a day."

"I can't think of anything, Chip. Did Robert stop by today? He said he might if time allowed."

"Yes, ma'am. He came by 'round two o'clock. He helped me out for 'bout an hour. I shore was happy 'bout that. Said he might stop by here again tomorrow."

"I know you are doing a great job, Chip, but still, it's always nice to have a little help now and then. Don't you agree?"

"Yes, ma'am, I won't argue that point."

"Well, I guess I'll see you at the breakfast table in the morning. Goodnight, Chip."

"Goodnight, ma'am," Chip said as he tipped the brim of his hat at her. He did an about-face and headed for the bunkhouse.

Connie was happy to hear that her brother, Robert, was helping Chip, and keeping an eye on things around the ranch. It could be somewhat overwhelming for someone as young as Chip to stay on top of everything.

Connie got Lena ready for bed, even though it was a bit early yet. She would select one of Lena's favorite children's storybooks and read to her.

As they sat down on the couch, Lena asked, "Is my daddy coming home today?"

"No, honey. Daddy is still working at a place far, far away from here. We must wait a few more days before he comes home to us. I know he wishes he could be here with you."

"Is Jesus taking care of my daddy?"

"Oh, yes, sweetie. Jesus is *always* watching over your daddy—just as he watches over you and me."

"I'm ready for my story now," Lena said, seemingly satisfied that all was well with the world—at least the part she was familiar with.

* * * * *

The meeting at Sugar Loaf Mountain ended around eight o'clock. The sun had long set. If it weren't for the numerous campfires, darkness would have ruled over the evening's meeting.

Captain O'Bryan and his group sat around their personal campfire talking about the meeting. They were glad that tomorrow would be a day of rest for everyone. The raid on Kantrell's hideout would not take place until Monday morning.

Clint expressed his concern to Jim that no more lawmen had shown up. He hoped that a few more would drift in on Sunday. His other companions shared the same hope. The current total of men consisted of thirty-four lawmen and one civilian leader, Mr. Henry Watts.

Clint, after conversing for a good while with his friends, departed their company to check on Apache. He was glad that his colt would not have to travel tomorrow. It would allow any soreness that his animal was experiencing to diminish. There was a small bottle of liniment in his saddlebag, if needed.

Satisfied that all was well with his steed, Clint returned to the campfire. He sat down next to Chino. He had never met the man before today—or his friend, Dewey. He rather liked them; however, there was something about each of them that was somewhat bothersome.

Chino was a husky sort of man, about thirty-five years of age, with sandy-blonde hair and a full beard. He wasn't quite six feet tall. He chewed tobacco, which greatly annoyed Clint, for it seemed like Chino had to spit a wad of nasty brown juice about every thirty seconds. The ground splatter was disgusting to Clint. Even the front of Chino's shirt was stained with tobacco juice.

Dewey, a slender man, was closer to forty years of age. He was shorter than Chino, had long brown hair, and—for the most part—was clean-shaven. Unfortunately, he was a heavy smoker. Clint did his very best to stay well upwind of him in order to breath healthier air.

"What are we gonna do tomorrow, Captain?" Dave asked as he poked a stick into the fire.

"We'll start by givin' our mounts a thorough inspection ... *and* ... our hardware, too. A dirty firearm could spell disaster," Jim said. "Other than that, gentlemen ... I ain't got a clue."

"Well, I'm gonna check out one of those big Saguaros," Clint revealed. "There's a good-sized one about hundred yards from here. It's got at least five arms on it."

"I saw some tall spiny-lookin' plants. Haven't a clue what they are," Titus said.

"Might be ocotillo," Clint guessed. "I usually ran across 'em when I traveled down to the Big Bend country."

"And what's 'em purty little trees with the *green* bark I see all over the place?" Titus asked.

"They are most likely Palo Verde," Mike answered, though he was not certain that that was exactly what Titus was referring to. "Point one out to me in the mornin' ... and I'll let ya know for certain if that's what ya are askin' me 'bout."

The conversations continued on for another hour or so. That's when Captain O'Bryan stood up, stretched his arms, and addressed his men. "Time to turn in, men," he ordered.

No one argued with his directive.

"*And*, gents, don't forget to check yer bedrolls for cute little desert critters," Mike reminded everyone. "Ya just never know what ya will find."

* * * * *

Not many miles away, at the base of Four Peaks, in Wild Burro Canyon, the conversations were winding down as well. The leader of the notorious gang of outlaws, Butch Kantrell, was making his way to one of the lean-tos to bed down for the night.

"Say, boss," began Russ Thorpe, "when did ya say we were leavin' this canyon?"

Russ was—along with a renegade Apache by the name of Two Scars—one of Kantrell's lieutenants. He was wanted in Texas and the New Mexico Territory for murder and cattle rustling. He was even wanted in Arkansas for stealing a horse. The price on his head had recently gone up to two thousand dollars.

Russ could not recall when he didn't live outside the law. Crime had been his life-style choice ever since he ran away from a Little Rock orphanage at the age of fifteen, stole a horse, and fled to Texas. He was now forty years old.

Kantrell turned about to face Thorpe. "Probably by mid-week," he replied, sounding a bit testy. "Are ya git'n nervous 'bout stayin' here?"

"Naw, I'm just anxious to see some new scenery," Thorpe lied. For he was indeed nervous about staying in one place too long. He felt that, sooner or later, the law would get word as to where they were hiding out. It didn't pay well to take root in any one place.

"Well, git yerself some sleep, and let me worry 'bout when we will move on. *Savvy?*"

"Right, Butch," said Thorpe, weakly. "Sorry I bothered ya."

Kantrell grunted and walked on to his lean-to.

Two Scars, the leathery-faced Apache, walked over and sat down next to Thorpe.

"What 'im say 'bout leavin' this place?"

"He said that we *might* pull out of here by mid-week."

"That not good. Must leave sooner. Lawmen find us before too many days if we stay here. Not safe here anymore."

"I know, Two Scars, but I'm not the one callin' the shots. It's best we keep our personal opinions to ourselves. Ya know how the boss can go off. He's got a very short fuse."

Two Scars grunted. "Me think boss not so wise. Maybe ya make better leader. Ya ever give much thought 'bout takin' over the gang?"

"Listen, I've been ridin' with Kantrell for ten years. So far, he's done a pretty good job of leadin' us," Thorpe said in defense of his boss.

"Hmmm. What ya say is true. Maybe me worry like old woman."

Thorpe gave off a half-hearted chuckle and said, "Yeah, maybe so."

Thorpe and Two Scars were the last to fill their bed-rolls. As far as they knew, nothing was on the agenda for tomorrow. It would be nice to have a day to rest—for a change.

No doubt, the citizens living in the surrounding countryside would enjoy a day free of raids by the outlaw gang even more so.

Chapter Eight

Sunday, October 11th.

Being primarily a rancher and not a lawman, Clint, as usual, was awake and out of his bedroll long before sunrise. There was barely a glimmer of light on the horizon as he walked over to the waning campfire and tossed on a couple of small logs.

Most lawmen probably didn't have to report to work until eight or nine o'clock. By nine o'clock, Clint, by and large, had all his horses watered, fed, and turned out to pasture.

Clint sat down by the campfire and pulled his wool blanket up around his shoulders to help fight off the morning chill.

As was his custom, Clint liked to read his Bible early in the morning—during a time of solitude. It somehow made his day a lot more manageable. He often compared the Bible to a roadmap, because it kept him moving forward in life on the appropriate trail.

Clint opened the small, frayed Bible and began his

meditation time by reading Psalm 100—his favorite. As he was finishing the last verse, Titus suddenly appeared from behind him.

"What ya be readin' Clint?" Titus asked in a low voice, so as not to wake the others. He already knew what Clint was reading, but he needed an opening for the rest of his questions.

"A roadmap to *victorious* living."

"Ya don't *really* believe everything that's written in that there book … do ya?"

"Yes, Titus, I most certainly do."

"All that Jesus stuff sounds rather made up to me. Kinda like one of 'em ol' dime novels."

"Titus, have you *any* sort of spiritual belief?" Clint asked as he was thumbing through the pages for a particular scripture verse. "Is there someone or somethin' that you do believe in?"

"Not really. If I did, it would be in myself. I figure every man is the ultimate ruler over his own existence. We are born, we do stuff, then we die," Titus matter-of-factly answered as he took a seat next to the veteran ranger.

"That sounds simple enough," Clint began, "providin', of course, that you want nothin' or expect nothin' after your earthly life comes to an end. As for me, I just happen to believe that the best part of my life will begin *after* I leave this ol' earth."

Clint paused, but Titus did not respond to his statement. *Maybe he's thinkin' over what I just said*, Clint thought.

"So, to you, who *is* Jesus?" Clint asked.

"Oh, I don't know. Just some good guy that roamed 'round the countryside tellin' folks how they should live their lives. And if they didn't do as he said, they would all end up in hell."

"Actually, my friend, He didn't just *tell* folks how to live a righteous life—He *showed* 'em how to live a righteous life by bein' an example to 'em. He could never be labeled a hypocrite."

"My uncle was a 'jack-leg' preacher of sorts ... and he shore didn't practice what he preached. He spent a good part of his life chasin' women and drinkin' 'til he passed out."

Clint let the comment pass. He continued with his line of questioning, being careful not to sound overly preachy.

"Titus, if I told you that you have an *eternal soul* livin' inside your body—would you know what I'm talkin' about?"

"Yeah, I guess so," Titus responded, though not entirely certain that he understood the concept. "Ain't it what makes me the person that I am?"

"Yeah, somethin' like that," Clint answered.

"But what do you mean by *eternal*?"

"After the body dies—the soul lives on forever."

"Hmmm, ya don't say?"

"Do you believe in hell, Titus? Or, for that matter, in heaven?"

"Naw, I don't reckon I do."

"So, if you died right this moment—where do you think your soul would end up?"

"In the ground along with my cold, stiff body ... and nobody would much care."

"God would certainly care. He loves you."

"Yeah, I'll just bet that's right," quipped Titus, somewhat sarcastically.

"And, because He loves you, He doesn't want to see your soul spend eternity in hell because of any sins you may have committed. That's why He sent His only son to die for your sins and my sins."

"I don't know 'bout no sins. I ain't never done all that much wrong," Titus uneasily replied.

"Really?" chirped Clint, his eyebrows rising.

Clint carefully formulated his next question in his mind before speaking. "If what you believe was wrong—would you be interested in knowin' about it?"

"Oh, I reckon I would, if it could be proven that I was wrong in my thinkin'."

Clint's finger was poised at Romans 3:23. "Would you mind if I read some verses to you?"

"Shore, why not. It can't hurt much."

"In the book of Romans it says: *'For all have sinned, and come short of the glory of God.'* That means none of us are without sin. None. To God, our sins are a really big deal."

"I doubt this god of yers cares much 'bout what I've done. He's gotta be too busy with bigger matters than to waste time worryin' 'bout the likes of me." Titus paused briefly. "Besides, I wouldn't say I was a *sinner.* I mean, I'm not perfect, but that don't make me a terrible person."

"Have you heard of the Ten Commandments?"

"Shore," Titus admitted, "who hasn't?"

"So, may I assume that you understand that the purpose of the Ten Commandments is to steer us from wrongful livin' ... and to expose our sins?"

"Yeah, I reckon I know a little somethin' 'bout that. But I never gave it much thought."

"Well, for just a moment, let's give it some thought.

110

I'd like to ask you a few more questions. Would that be okay with you?"

"Shore, why not."

"To begin with—have you ever claimed somethin' to be true that you knew wasn't true?"

"I've told a little *white* lie now and then."

"Then, accordin' to God's Word, you've sinned by bearin' false witness."

Clint paused.

"Have you ever cheated someone out of his or her property—or perhaps swiped somethin' that you hadn't paid for?"

"Yeah, I cheated at poker a few times. And, a few years back, I swiped some jerked beef from a general store," Titus reluctantly confessed.

"When you cheated at cards and stole the jerky—did you feel that it was wrong?"

"I reckon. But, hey, I didn't git caught."

"No matter—accordin' to God's Word, Titus, you've sinned by stealin'."

Titus remained silent.

"You're a single man, right?" Clint asked.

"Yeah," Titus said. "Never been hitched."

"So, my friend, have you ever been with a woman in an intimate way?"

Titus hesitated a moment before giving his answer to such a delicate question.

"Yeah, I reckon I have," Titus said as he hung his head low. "I've been known to visit Maggie's bordello in Flag' whenever I'm up that way. It's no big deal—right? I mean, ya know, a man's gotta have a little fun now and then—don't he?"

"First Thessalonians, chapter four, says that it is

111

God's will that you should avoid sexual immorality. God calls it *fornication.*"

"I ain't ever heard that word before," Titus said as he scratched at his cheek. "It really says that?"

"Yes, it does. So, let's review your answers, okay? So far, you've admitted to being a *liar,* a *thief,* and a *fornicator.* Have I missed anything?"

"Hey! Th-that's not very fair!" Titus protested, though he knew the accusations were warranted.

Clint quickly turned the pages to Romans 6:23. "Paul, an apostle, and the writer of Romans, had this to say: *'For the wages of sin is death; but the gift of God is eternal life through Jesus Christ our Lord.'* Paul is sayin' that sin brings with it eternal separation from God—if it isn't dealt with. We must repent."

Clint flipped back the pages to Romans 5:8. "Let me read another verse. *'But God commendeth his love toward us, in that, while we were yet sinners, Christ died for us.'* This is sayin' that God loves us so much that He allowed His own son, who was without sin, to die with *our* sins heaped upon Him. Why? Because He wants us to enjoy eternity with Him in His kingdom."

"I remember when I was a kid, my grandmother would read to me that John 3:16 verse. I reckon I never got it out of my head," Titus admitted.

"But, did you believe it?"

"I reckon I did—for a while."

"What changed your mind?"

"I don't know. Life got tough later on. I figured if there was a god, and he claimed to love me so much, he wouldn't let bad things happen to me."

"It's the bad things that God allows in our life that makes us strong, Titus. If life were all rosy and sweet, your faith would never be tested. How would you ever know you had *real* faith—the kind of faith that can move a mountain?"

"Well, I guess that makes sense."

Clint turned ahead to Romans 10:9,10. "Paul had this to say: *'That if thou shalt confess with thy mouth the Lord Jesus, and shalt believe in thine heart that God hath raised Him from the dead, thou shalt be saved. For with the heart man believeth unto righteousness; and with the mouth confession is made unto salvation.'* It's a matter of the heart—not the mind."

"Well, there's no way I could ask God to forgive me and save me from hell. I've got to clean up my act first. Maybe after I've been livin' right for awhile."

"That won't work, Titus. There is nothin' you can do on your own that would make you clean enough or acceptable enough to God. *¡Nada!* Nothin'! Zip! Zero!

"There is only one way for you and me to enter the gates of heaven. Jesus said: *'I am the way and the truth and the life. No one comes to the Father except through me.'* That means that your feeble efforts to clean up your life on your own are not gonna help you one tiny bit."

"Are ya shore 'bout that?"

"Absolutely! It's like this: if you could save yourself from hell by doin' good works, then you've taken Jesus completely out of the picture. Paul, in his epistle to the church at Ephesus, wrote that it is by *grace* that we are saved, and not by our works. That grace comes only from Christ Jesus.

"The writer of Romans says: *'For whosoever shall call upon the name of the Lord shall be saved.'* That's all you've got to do."

"It says that?"

"Yes, it does. Think for a moment, Titus. Is there any logical reason at all that you would not want to receive His love and forgiveness?"

"So, ya are sayin' that if I git myself killed one of these days, I'm headin' straight to hell—no matter what I try to do on my own to fix things today?

"That if I don't confess belief in Jesus—or ask Him to forgive me and save me—I ain't got a prayer of seein' heaven?"

"Couldn't have said it better myself. Our good works don't buy us one square inch of heaven. However, once you've become a 'born again' believer—things immediately change—your good works will count for somethin' then. There will come a day when *believers* will be rewarded for their good works."

"I still don't see how a god that supposedly loves me can send me to hell. It doesn't make sense."

"It is God's heartfelt desire that you spend eternity in heaven. It will be by your own 'free will' that you *choose* to go to hell. God can't force you to love Him. You must, in your heart, *want* to love Him. The choice is totally yours."

"I gotta think on all this salvation stuff for a spell, Clint. I'll git back to ya."

"That's pretty much what Governor Felix said to Paul in the Book of Acts. It's a worthy story."

"Huh? Well, reckon I ain't heard that tale."

"It's no tale. I'll tell you about it sometime—if there *is* a sometime."

"Now ya are tryin' to scare me! Stop that!"

"No, I'm not the one scarin' you—that's your conscience workin' on you. Some of what I have said is stickin'. Praise God for that. There's a verse that says:

'Men perish because they refuse to love the truth and so be saved.' Please, don't reject the truth."

Titus shook his head, stood up, and walked away. Clint closed his Bible and began to pray for his lost friend.

Several minutes later, Clint walked over to where his horse was tethered. He freed him from the picket line and walked him about for several minutes. Apache showed no signs of being sore in his joints. Clint wished he could say the same thing about himself. His lower back was still bothering him—but not as bad as yesterday.

When Clint returned to the campfire, he found Jim sitting close to the fire pit. He was warming his hands over the low flames. The others were still in their bed-rolls. Titus had wandered off without saying where he was going. Clint hoped he was spending time thinking over all that he had said to him earlier.

"Good mornin', Jim."

"Mornin', Clint. Sleep well?"

"Pretty much. My back is still a bit sore."

"Sorry to hear that," replied Jim, sincerely. "Are you ready for some coffee?"

"Do you need to ask me that?" Clint said with a chuckle. "Do birds need wings?"

"Wings don't do *emus* much good."

Clint laughed. He liked Jim. He always knew what to expect from him. *If I had another brother, I'd want him to be just like Jim*, he thought.

Clint's mind suddenly opened up to thoughts of his brother, Chad, and how an outlaw named Wayne Carver had killed his brother several years ago. At the time, Chad was a peace officer in San Angelo, Texas.

"You okay, Clint?" Jim asked. "You suddenly got a strange look on your face."

"Oh, yeah, I'm fine. My mind momentarily drifted back to an unpleasant incident that happened a long time ago in Texas."

"Want to talk about it?"

"Oh, no. I'd rather focus on happier times."

"Coffee should be ready in a minute or two."

"I can hardly wait," Clint said as he looked at the others still slumbering in their bedrolls. "Should I wake 'em, or let 'em snooze a while longer?"

"Yeah, go ahead and roust 'em out of the sack. It's almost eight o'clock."

Clint went from tent to tent waking up his fellow rangers and Marshal Chandler. None were too happy with him—and freely expressed it.

"Where's Titus?" Jim asked.

"I was talkin' to him earlier. I'll go look for him."

Clint walked over to the main tent and saw Titus talking with three men. They were the same three young deputies that rode in late yesterday afternoon.

Clint approached them.

"What's up, Clint?" Titus asked.

"Oh nothin', much. Captain O'Bryan got concerned when he didn't see you at our campsite," Clint replied. "I'll let him know where you're at. I hope you'll pardon my intrusion?"

"Before ya go, allow me to introduce these nice fellers to ya."

After the introductions were completed, Clint excused himself and returned to his own campsite.

"Did you find 'im?" Jim asked.

"Yep. He's over by the main tent talkin' to those three deputies that rode in here late yesterday."

"Those young lookin' ones?"

"Yeah. They seemed friendly enough."

Once everyone was up and ready to eat, Clint started breakfast for the group. Titus had returned and was drinking coffee with Geoff, Dave, Chino, Dewey and Mike. Jim was assisting Clint with the meal preparations.

A little later, as they were sitting around the campfire finishing up their meal, Titus began to speak about his encounter with the three youthful deputies.

"Them deputies are out of Mesa City. And git this—they are brothers! Luke, Matthew and John Domann."

"Ha! Sounds almost biblical—like your name—*Titus*," Clint cheerfully commented. "It wouldn't surprise me none if there's another brother back at the house by the name of *Mark*."

"They didn't say nothin' 'bout no Mark."

Clint's rather off-the-cuff comment—meant to be witty—apparently sailed over Titus' head. He failed to grasp Clint's biblical association.

"It kinda reminds me of the time when the Earp brothers were marshalin' down in Tombstone," Chino observed. "Reckon most of 'em is dead now, 'cept for ol' Wyatt."

"Wonder where Wyatt is these days?" Jim said.

"I hear tell he went to Alaska," Clint answered.

"Well, I heard he was livin' in California," Mike interjected, "with some theatrical lady."

"Reckon he was a close friend of Doc Holliday," Dewey added. "Is Holliday dead?"

"Don't rightly know," Clint replied. "Last I read about him, he was mighty sick with consumption."

Captain O'Bryan stood up and cleared his throat. It got everyone focused on him.

"Gentlemen, I think, in the next hour or so, we should mosey over to the main tent and say 'howdy' to anyone we haven't met yet. I rather like knowin' what kinda men I'm fightin' alongside of in a battle."

"Yeah, good idea, Jim," Clint agreed. "It would certainly give us some idea of the experience level of our soon-to-be companions."

The lawmen finished their breakfast, cleaned up their dishes, and checked on their horses. Once the horses were fed and watered, they moseyed over to the main tent to mingle with their peers. They visited for about two hours.

It was obvious to all that they were shorthanded. The odds weren't good. It was likely, by Monday afternoon, one or more of them would probably not be among the living.

The day seemed to fly by. A lot of ideas were exchanged on how the raid should come off. Henry Watts briefed everyone again on the details of the campaign. He wanted to ensure that everyone was on the same page.

Clint even found time during the day to wander in the desert and check out a giant Saguaro cactus. It was about thirty feet high with five large arms. He was amazed by its texture as he felt it.

Sadly, while investigating the desert giant, he managed to get a segment of Cholla stuck to his leg. It easily penetrated his heavy cotton denims. It was a painful experience, to say the least. Mike showed Clint how to remove the Cholla safely by using the large end of a comb to extract it from his leg. "Never use yer fingers to remove Cholla!" Mike was careful to warn his friend.

It was now shortly after sunset, and Clint was sitting alone several feet from the campfire nursing his sore leg when Titus approached and sat down near him.

"Are ya busy, Clint?"

"No, not at all," he said, while rubbing some of the horse liniment on his reddened leg.

"I guess that Cholla can be plenty painful, huh?"

"Oh, yeah! And I had to find out the hard way."

"Clint, what do I gotta do to become one of them 'born again' believers?"

"It's really quite simple, Titus. Do you admit that you're a sinner?"

"Yeah, I do."

"Do you truly want forgiveness of your sins?"

"Yes, sir, I really do."

"Do you believe that Christ Jesus died for you on a cross ... and that it took His shed blood to wash away your sins ... and not your feeble works? And, do you believe that He was resurrected from the grave ... and is alive today?"

"Yes," Titus nodded, "to all yer questions."

"Are you now willin' to accept Christ Jesus as Savior and Lord of your life? And, are you willin' to surrender your life to Him and obey His teachings?"

"Again, yes, to all yer questions."

"Are you now ready to invite the Savior of the world into your life?"

"Yes, Clint, I'm ready to do just that."

"Then let's pray together the *believer's* prayer."

Clint reached out and put his right hand on Titus' left

shoulder. Both men knelt down and bowed their heads. Clint led the prayer as Titus repeated the words. A moment later, they were finished. Clint gave his new *brother in Christ* an animated and joyful slap-on-the-back hug. "The angels are rejoicing, Titus."

"I can't explain it, Clint, but I really do feel different. I don't have all that heavy burden of sin weighin' me down any longer. I now know that if I should die—I'll be with the Lord forever. The worry of death has completely fled from my mind."

"Bein' a believer isn't easy, Titus. The devil will be after you in a rage from here on out. You'll fail at times—we all do. But now you've got the Holy Spirit stickin' up for you. Follow the Spirit's lead and you'll come out on the other side with your crown of victory untarnished."

"I'll do my best, sir," Titus said. "And, sir, would ya mind if I borrowed yer Good Book for a spell?"

"Not at all. I'll fetch it for you."

Titus followed Clint to his tent.

Clint rummaged about in his saddlebag for a brief moment and produced the tattered Bible.

"You'll want to read, foremost, the Gospel of John, Titus. It will educate you faster than any other book as to who our Lord Jesus is ... and His divine plan for your life."

"Thanks, Clint."

Clint smiled and nodded his head as he turned about to go back to the campfire. Titus fell in behind the veteran ranger. Titus sat down close to the fire so as to benefit from its emanating light. He flipped the pages over until he reached the Gospel of John. *Well, Lord, here we go*, he thought to himself. *Lay your message on my heart*, he inwardly prayed.

A moment or two later, Clint interrupted Titus.

"If you have any questions—don't hesitate to ask me for help. Okay?"

"Will do, Clint. Thanks."

Clint stood and moved away from Titus to give him some privacy as he read. He decided to check on Apache before it got any darker. There was scarcely any daylight left on the western horizon. Darkness may engulf the campsite, but Clint had the satisfaction of knowing that there was now no "darkness" in the heart of Titus. The "light" of the Holy Spirit now resided there.

Jim waited a few moments before approaching Clint. "What's goin' on with our young ranger?"

"Another soul has been snatched from the grip of the devil," Clint was quick to proclaim.

"Praise God for that!" Jim exclaimed as he slapped Clint on the back. "Chalk one up for Jesus' team. The more the merrier."

Clint smiled.

"By chance, are you sure you didn't miss your calling—*Pastor* Wells?"

"I don't think so, Jim. As you know, it's the job of *every* believer to spread the gospel. I'm just obeyin' Jesus' command," Clint humbly answered. "I just planted the seed, the Holy Spirit does the waterin', and God does the harvestin'."

"Amen to that!" Jim concluded.

* * * * *

"Men," Kantrell began as he stood up, "in a couple of days we are gonna ride out of this here canyon. I feel we need some new scenery."

121

Immediately, there arose a low rumble of voices from the large group of outlaws in attendance for Kantrell's unexpected announcement. Most of the men seemed to be in agreement with their leader.

"I haven't made up my mind, just yet, as to where we'll go, but I'm guessin' south to Tucson or maybe even a bit closer to the border.

"I think we've probably worn out our welcome in these parts," he concluded with a slight snicker.

There were more low rumblings and a few chuckles, as well.

"I spotted some of you nodding in agreement. Are there any here that don't feel like we should go?"

Many of the men turned about to scan the crowd, including Russ Thorpe and Two Scars, but no one spoke up.

"Well, then it's settled—we leave in two days."

Kantrell sat back down. "That's all I have to say—for now."

Russ Thorpe stood up and walked over to where his boss was sitting.

Kantrell looked up at him and said, "Are ya happy now?"

"What do ya mean, Butch?"

"I know ya was git'n worried 'bout bein' here so long. Can't fool me none."

"Yeah, I suppose I was at that," Thorpe finally admitted. "It just makes sense to me to move on before the law gets wind of where we've been hidin' out."

"Ya don't have to explain yerself," Kantrell said rather sourly. "Tell the men to turn in. We've got a lot to do tomorrow. I want to make another raid before we head out. We'll need some supplies for our trip."

"Yes, sir," Thorpe replied.

As soon as Thorpe had departed, Kantrell stood up and walked off into the darkness to contemplate the raids that would take place the next day. He knew that they had just about run out of places to raid.

Hmmm, perhaps Mesa City is plenty ripe for pickin'? he pondered quietly to himself.

Chapter Nine

Monday, October 12th.

An hour after sunrise, two riders suddenly appeared on the ridge above the sprawling camp. They paused momentarily before riding down the hill toward the main tent. Henry Watts greeted them warmly after they dismounted, then quickly escorted them inside his tent.

"What do ya make of that?" asked Dave Martin, addressing his boss.

"Not sure. They were not wearin' badges," Captain Jim O'Bryan declared to his veteran ranger.

"If they're with us—that makes a total of thirty-seven. But, that's still a long way from the number of men we need," Clint Wells said as he took another sip of coffee from his well-stained cup.

Jim looked irritated. "How right you are," he grunted. "I guess it wasn't all that important to *every* community to support the governor's mandate."

"It shore do look that way, Cap'," remarked Geoff

Tingle. "Not a single lawman showed up here on Sunday. No, sir, not even one."

"As soon as y'all finish your breakfast, we'll mosey over to the main tent and find out what's goin' on," Jim said.

Twenty minutes later, Captain O'Bryan and his personal group of men joined the others at the main tent. Mr. Watts soon exited his tent with the two new arrivals. These two men represented his 'ace-in-the-hole.' The governor's envoy cleared his throat and addressed the crowd before him.

"Lawmen of this here Arizona Territory, please give me your attention. Today, we ride against Kantrell's gang of robbers and murderers. Our goal is to bring law and order to this beautiful territory of ours. We are about to embark on a campaign that is very necessary and also very dangerous. It's no secret that we are shorthanded. I was expecting fifty or more of your caliber to show up, but sadly, that hasn't happened.

"Standing here with me are two veteran lawmen that have been at the Kantrell hideout, working undercover, for the past two months. They have just briefed me on the situation there. We will be up against a gang of forty-seven hardcore outlaws. Many are wanted in other areas of the country, but have come here to escape justice.

"Today, gentlemen, Kantrell and his men will face the justice that they have tried to avoid for a very long time. Moments from now, we will ride out of here. These two undercover agents will leave immediately, and ride back to Kantrell's hideout and take out the sentries that are guarding the entrance to Wild Burro Canyon. Once Kantrell's sentries are eliminated, we can move in and set up strategic positions on the ridges overlooking his encampment. That should give us the upper hand that we so sorely need."

Henry Watts paused to catch his breath.

"Any questions?" Mr. Watts asked, while scanning the faces before him. "None? Then begin your preparations."

The two undercover agents mounted up and departed the camp. Their mission was vital. Taking out the sentries would allow their fellow lawmen to approach Kantrell's hideout without being detected. Thirty-five horses would, no doubt, create a large dust cloud that could be seen for miles.

It was a five-mile ride to Kantrell's canyon hideaway. The biggest problem would be navigating the narrow, rocky trail. The lawmen would have to ride in single file. Venture off the trail, even a little bit, and you could find yourself brushing up against one of several different species of Cholla and other painful varieties of cacti. Of the seventy-four native species of Arizona cacti, nearly half of them could be found in the area of Four Peaks. Even the three-inch needle-sharp thorns of the mesquite could cause injury to both man and beast.

There was also the danger of a horse stepping into a borrow hole due to a single careless maneuver. If the horse stumbled and broke a leg, the rider could be catapulted to his death. Furthermore, a screaming horse could be heard for a mile or two—easily alerting the outlaws.

As soon as they were ready, Captain O'Bryan and his group led their horses over to the main tent. It appeared that everyone was ready to depart. When Mr. Watts saw the leader of the rangers approaching, he motioned for him to come closer.

"Those 'railroad tracks' (slang for captain bars) on your lapel indicate to me, Captain O'Bryan, that you are the ranking lawman in this camp. There are no United States marshals represented here. We have two sheriffs on station, but they don't outrank an officer in the ranger corp. The majority of our force is made up of sheriff deputies and town marshals or their town deputies. That being the case, I want you to ride up front with me as my second-in-command."

"Yes, sir. I'd be honored to do that."

"Captain, if something unfortunate should happen to me, you will take over as leader of this company of men. Is that understood?"

"Yes, sir. I completely understand."

Henry Watts turned about to address the entire group that stood before him.

"I want it made clear to each of you—this will be your leader if I'm severely wounded or killed. Is there an objection?"

"What if somethin' happens to Captain O'Bryan?" asked a deputy at the back of the group.

"The ranking sheriff here is Bob McDowell, from the Phoenix office," Mr. Watts promptly replied. "Sheriff McDowell—raise your hand up high so everyone can see you."

Sheriff McDowell raised his hand and turned about so everyone could see his face. He quickly turned back to see if Henry Watts had anything more to say.

"And before you ask, our next ranking officer is Sheriff Tim Hayden, from Casa Grande. Sheriff Hayden—raise your hand up high for all to see. Now then, you all know who to look to for leadership. God forbid that we lose anyone."

"Sir," Jim began, "we have another ca—"

Jim suddenly espied Clint out of the corner of his eye. He was frantically signaling for him to stop speaking.

"Yes, Captain?" Mr. Watts said as he turned his attention to Jim. "What were you about to say?"

"Never mind, sir. It can wait," Jim said as he glanced at Clint with a puzzled expression.

Mr. Watts addressed the group once again.

"Gentlemen, I've got two more points to make: first point, the trail is very rough—so keep a steady rein on your mounts; second point, absolutely no talking once we pick up the trailhead—for voices can carry a long distance in the desert."

Mr. Watts paused and scanned the group.

"That's all I have to say, for now. Mount up!"

The excitement began to boil over. The lawmen were anxious and feeling the tension. It seemed the horses were picking up on this excitement and tension, as well. Several horses were prancing about and snorting. As Clint raised his left leg to insert his foot in the stirrup, Apache quickly moved away. Clint tried again to mount his colt—same end result. It took Clint a minute to calm down his young colt and get mounted.

As soon as everyone was ready, the lawmen, in single file, rode up and over the ridge to the main stage road. Just before he reached the top of the ridge, Clint looked back at all the campsites. He hoped there wouldn't be any empty bedrolls tonight. The only men left behind were the four personal aides to Henry Watts—all were civilians.

Riding directly behind Clint was his fellow ranger, Titus Green. "Titus, how are you feelin' this mornin'?"

"*Saved*, my brother!"

"Praise the Lord!" Clint said jubilantly.

Titus nodded. "Ya can say that again!"

Clint counted the number of riders in front of him. There were nine. Up front was the governor's envoy, Henry Watts. Directly behind Mr. Watts were Captain Jim O'Bryan, Sheriff Bob McDowell, and five other lawmen that Clint did not know by name.

Sheriff Tim Hayden was riding directly in front of Clint. And, as was previously mentioned, directly behind Clint was Titus.

Behind Titus were Geoff Tingle, Dave Martin and Mike Chandler. And behind Mike were Chino Watson, Dewey Loomis and nineteen other riders.

The three Domann brothers were among those nineteen riders, and they were positioned near the tail end of the procession.

Once on the stage road, the riders fanned out, and even rode three or four abreast. It was about a half-mile ride to the trailhead that led to the outlaws' hideaway. This would be the last chance anyone would have to talk to each other.

Captain O'Bryan decided to address his friends and fellow rangers while he had the opportunity.

"Men," he began, "we are fixin' to ride through hell. God have mercy on each of you. And knowin' Clint as I do, he has already prayed for God's protection over you. And I confess—so have I."

"And just so y'all know—last night Clint led me to Jesus. Today, I ride into battle without the worry of where I'll spend eternity if somethin' should happen to me," Titus proudly confessed.

"That's wonderful!" Mike replied.

Jim, Geoff and Dave expressed their delight as well.

Captain O'Bryan maneuvered his mount closer to Clint Wells. He had a burning question on his mind.

"Clint, why did you stop me from tellin' Watts about you bein' a captain?"

"Well, I figure we got ourselves plenty of chiefs and so few Indians. Besides, I could tell Sheriff McDowell was itchin' to be 'top dog' of this outfit."

"Huh, I never even considered *his* feelings. You're a very thoughtful person, Clint."

A few minutes later the riders reached the trailhead. Henry Watts called for silence. Everyone lined up as they were before and reined their mounts off of the main road and onto the narrow trail.

The trail to the outlaws' hideout was barely forty inches wide. It was strewn with small, sharp stones. Broken segments of needle-sharp Cholla were lying all about. If the segments were disturbed, they would literally "jump" from their resting place and embed themselves in a horse's leg. The result would be highly painful. (As Clint could readily attest to—if asked.)

One of the greatest fears each rider shared was having their horse spook, rear up, and toss them off onto a full-grown Cholla or a clump of prickly pear cactus. The pain would be like that of a thousand scorpion stings—though not as fatal.

The riders rode slowly and carefully. Things were progressing well. *So far—so good*, Clint thought. Even though he was watching the trail, Clint could not help but scan his surroundings. The desert was a beautiful place, and Clint was taking it all in. He didn't know when he would ever see it again. How something so beautiful could be so dangerous was a mystery to him.

Four Peaks was now rising up thousands of feet above them. It took Clint's breath away. They were magnificent peaks, each peak reaching high for the clouds. He was glad the outlaws hadn't posted sentries on top of one of the saddles between the peaks. If they had, their approach would already be detected.

After riding up, over, and then down several low ridges, and crossing several sandy washes—they came to a point were they could see the narrow opening that led into a wide canyon located in the shadow of Four Peaks. Henry Watts raised his hand to bring the procession to a halt. He was waiting for a signal from one of his undercover agents that indicated that the sentries were eliminated. That signal would come in the form of a mirror reflecting sunlight.

Henry Watts dismounted, and signaled with a hand jester for his entourage to do the same. As the men were dismounting, a flash of light streaked several times across their position. It was from one of the undercover agents. The way was clear to proceed.

The governor's man sent Sheriff McDowell back among the ranks with instructions to secure the horses in an arroyo near where they were standing. From here on, all forward movement would be on foot. It was nearly five hundred yards to the mouth of the box canyon, requiring a gradual uphill climb all the way.

Earlier that morning, the two undercover agents had indicated that there were several strategic locations along the upper rim of the canyon where men could set up firing positions and be fairly well protected by boulders. Clint prayed that that was indeed the case.

It took several minutes, but the thirty-five horses were finally secured in a safe place. Four men were assigned to stay with the horses. They were a mix of sheriff deputies and town deputies—the very youngest ones. However, not a single one of the three Domann brothers was among them. Each brother had flatly refused to be left behind with the horses.

With rifles, carbines, pistols, and extra boxes of cartridges at the ready, a group of thirty lawmen waited for the order from their civilian leader to march on the outlaw encampment. Mr. Watts walked quietly among them and shook each hand. Lastly, he pointed at his canteen and indicated that each man should take water. Most had their canteen, but a few had to go back to their horse and retrieve it.

It was Mr. Watts' intention to split up his men and position a team of shooters on the north ridge and south ridge of the canyon; thereby, putting the outlaws in a crossfire situation.

Both undercover agents had described the canyon as

being approximately two hundred yards long, and one hundred yards wide—with only one exit. The three side-walls of the canyon were not very high, perhaps two hundred feet or less; nonetheless, the angle of the walls was too steep for a horse to climb up—even without a rider. However, a man afoot could easily climb out and escape.

Mr. Watts planned to take up a position at the entrance to the canyon. He would have six men with him. If any outlaw should try to escape the canyon, they would ride into a wall of hot lead.

The two undercover agents would remain at their current sentry posts (three hundred yards from the mouth of the canyon) to watch the back trail. The agents weren't entirely certain if all forty-seven outlaws were still in the canyon.

Using hand signals, Mr. Watts split up the remaining group of lawmen. He wished now that he hadn't left four men with the horses. *Two would have been adequate,* he thought.

Captain O'Bryan would lead his group of men up the right ridge of the canyon. He would keep all of his rangers with him. He did not want to lose sight of them. As it turned out, his group also included Marshal Chandler and the three Domann brothers from Mesa City. In all, he was leading eleven men.

Sheriff McDowell would take his group of men up the left ridge. In all, he, too, was leading eleven men, which included Sheriff Hayden.

Mr. Watts gave the signal to move out. The right group made their way up the gentle, but rocky slope to its terminus. They were now approximately one hundred feet higher than where they had started. The same was roughly true for the left group.

The lawmen peered down into the canyon. What they saw was a large corral at the back of the canyon. It was fenced in on three sides. The canyon wall formed the fourth side. There were also five large, makeshift lean-tos. Each lean-to was framed up with a large vertical post at each corner, with each post connected to the other by smaller horizontal posts. Heavy hemp rope was looped from front to back to form rafters for the flat canvas roof. The shelters were crude at best, but effective.

Besides the lean-tos and the corral, dozens of armed men were milling about the canyon floor. They seemed totally oblivious to the lawmen lying prone on the ridges above them.

Henry Watts walked bravely to the mouth of the canyon with his small group of men. He took a deep breath, exhaled slowly, and geared up to introduce himself to Butch Kantrell.

"Kantrell! It's the law! Lay down your weapons and surrender!"

Straight away, the outlaw encampment was filled with frantic commotion. Following a seemingly long delay, a lone voice finally challenged the governor's envoy.

"Who are ya?! What do ya want?!" Kantrell yelled back, his voice laced with antagonism.

"My name is Henry Watts! I'm here on behalf of the governor—with men from every level of law enforcement to arrest you and your men! I have a legal warrant!"

"Take yer warrant and shove it!" Kantrell bellowed. "Ya better ride out of here while ya still got yer hides attached to yer bodies!"

"Threats will not do you any good!" Mr. Watts warned. "I've got you surrounded on all sides! There is no way out but through me and my well-armed men!"

Kantrell knew he was trapped like a caged cougar. He wasn't sure if he should give in or fight his way out. He would try to beg for some time to think things over.

"Well, *Henry,* me and the boys ain't shore how we want to play out this little game of yers. We'd like some time to talk among ourselves ... and vote on what we ought to do 'bout yer intrusion!"

"Fair enough! You've got ten minutes to decide if you want to come out peacefully, or turn this canyon into a bloody battlefield!"

"I'll give ya my answer—in ten minutes!"

Kantrell immediately scattered his men throughout the canyon floor. All were now fully armed and poised for action.

Clint looked at Jim. Jim shook his head. They both knew this wasn't going to end peacefully. "He's just buyin' time to form his plan to cut out," Clint surmised.

"You're absolutely right, Clint," agreed Jim, wholeheartedly.

Kantrell gathered his two top cronies to himself for a quick powwow.

One was Russ Thorpe, primarily a rustler of cattle, but a murderer as well. He had killed six men in his lifetime—two in Texas and four in the New Mexico Territory. So far, he had not killed anyone in Arizona, but he had come close to doing so on more than one occasion.

The other was a renegade Apache by the name of Two Scars. No one knew his age, but he looked to be in his thirties. He had killed a countless number of white settlers throughout most of central and southern Arizona. The military had spent the past nine months searching for him. And here he was—not quite eighty yards via a rifle bullet from where Clint lay prone on the upper right rim of the canyon.

"Hey, Captain," Chino began, "that's Two Scars down there. The military has been lookin' for 'im under every rock in the territory."

"Clint," Jim began, "you're the best shot we've got on this side of the canyon. Do ya think ya can take 'im out—*if* and *when* we get the word?"

"From this distance—not a problem."

"Get 'im lined up in your sights," Jim ordered.

Clint's Winchester .44-.40 rifle had a long barrel that was octagon shaped for more resistance to heat buildup. It even boasted an extra rear sight that made it deadly accurate at long range. But the feature Clint liked most was its twelve round capacity—four more rounds than a common carbine.

Clint peered down the barrel. He had the front sight focused dead center on Two Scars' heart. He felt a bead of sweat run down his temple, but his hands were steady. He was very adroit in these situations.

The minutes continued to tick down. Every palm was sweating from anticipation. Clint had to rub his eye several times to keep it in focus.

Down below, the lawmen could see the powwow that was in progress. It appeared to Jim that some of the outlaws were moving closer to the corral.

"Hmmm, I think they're git'n all fired up to abandon ship," he said to those closest to him.

"Yeah, it shore do look that way, Captain," agreed Chino.

"Gents, fix your sights on those men that are fallin' back toward the corral," Jim ordered. "Have you still got Two Scars in your sights, Clint?"

"I'm fixed on 'im, Jim."

"Two minutes to go," announced Jim.

On the canyon floor, Kantrell and his two lieutenants had come to a consensus. It was time to let Henry Watts know what they had agreed on.

Kantrell walked closer to the mouth of the canyon so that Mr. Watts could clearly hear him. Fifty yards behind him were Thorpe and Two Scars. Both were seeking cover in the rocks. It was a clear indication to the lawmen that something terrible was about to happen.

"Ya prove to be the wiser man, Thorpe," Two Scars said as he backed up closer to a large boulder. "We should have left here many days ago."

"Yeah, we certainly should have. But little does it matter now," said Thorpe, sourly.

"Ya think we make it out of here alive?"

"Maybe," Thorpe replied with a bit more civility in his voice. "They've got the high ground ... and it won't be easy defendin' our position."

"That true. Apache always protect high ground, but Kantrell say it not necessary. Him wrong. Me think 'im a fool."

"Well, my friend, if we are lucky enough to git out of this situation alive—ya tell 'im that." Thorpe's speech was caustic once again.

"Ya afraid of Kantrell?"

"Right this minute, I'm only afraid of dyin' long before my time."

"Me think this whole deal is *mucho* bad medicine," Two Scars said as he summed up the current situation.

"That's an *understatement* if I ever heard one," Thorpe quipped.

"What that mean?" asked Two Scars.

"I'll explain it to ya one of these days," Thorpe answered, his voice still caustic.

Two Scars merely grunted as he levered a round into his somewhat battered carbine.

Butch Kantrell was now in position near the mouth of the canyon. He was ready to deliver his answer to Henry Watts. He was feeling apprehensive. Woefully, he now realized that he had made a big mistake by staying in Wild Burro Canyon too long. He never dreamed that the law would discover his hiding place so soon.

On the ridge, high above the canyon floor, Jim looked at his watch. Kantrell's time was up. The stage was now set. It appeared to the lawmen that surrender was not going to be a part of Kantrell's overall strategy.

Jim felt tense. "Clint, are you still focused on Two Scars?" he asked.

"He's movin' around a lot, Jim, but I've still got 'im in my sights," affirmed Clint.

"There are several of 'em ol' boys standin' just outside the corral, Cap'," Geoff said as he adjusted his body to get more comfortable.

"They'll be wantin' to mount up as soon as the shootin' starts," Dave surmised.

"I'd say you are dead on with that assessment," Clint added.

"I don't have a watch, but I'd say that ten minutes has come and gone, Captain," Titus commented.

"Over a minute ago," Clint replied. "I reckon Watts is being a bit generous with his time."

Jim glanced across the canyon to see if Sheriff McDowell and his men were in place. They were. Jim gave a quick wave to McDowell. He quickly returned the wave. Everyone was prepared.

"Get ready men, it's fixin' to break loose any second

now!" Jim warned as he wiped a bead of sweat from his right temple.

Chapter Ten

Ten minutes later.

"Your time is up, Kantrell. Drop your weapons and come out with your hands high in the air! There doesn't have to be any blood spilled here today!" shouted Mr. Watts.

Kantrell's reply came quickly. "It's either spill blood or swing from the end of a hangman's rope! Surrendering isn't much of an option for the likes of us! I think we'll pass on yer offer!"

"Sorry to hear that, Kantrell! You leave us no other option but to come in there and take you out—one way or another!" threatened Mr. Watts.

Captain O'Bryan detected the obvious and hastily alerted his men. "Get ready, it's about to start. Pick your targets carefully ... and make every shot count. We can't afford to waste ammunition."

Suddenly, without forewarning, a single shot ricocheted off a boulder just inches from where Mr. Watts was standing. Fragments from the boulder pelted the sleeve of his suit coat. He promptly ducked for cover. Seconds later, several more shots rang out from the canyon floor. So far, no shots had been fired by any of the lawmen. Earlier, Mr. Watts had given strict orders not to fire on the outlaws until he gave the prearranged signal.

Jim grunted and angrily spouted, "What in thunder is Watts waitin' on?"

"Perhaps a written invitation!" quipped Clint.

The gunfire suddenly stopped as quickly as it started. The lawmen were puzzled by this unnatural action by wanted outlaws. Mr. Watts took the opportunity to speak to Kantrell one more time.

"Kantrell! Are you *sure* this is how you want it to play out?! I can't restrain my men much longer!"

His question was answered with another volley of rapid fire aimed at him and at the high places to his left and to his right. Mr. Watts was now satisfied that he had given the unrepentant outlaw leader every possible chance. He gave the signal to fire.

The lawmen opened up on the horde of wanted men below. Four outlaws reeled back and fell over dead; two others were wounded but kept on firing at their pursuers.

Clint never got a chance to take out Two Scars. When the first few shots rang out, the Apache leaped behind a large boulder, where he was now sufficiently hidden from view.

Chaos was the order of things in the makeshift corral where the outlaws' horses were being kept. It appeared that at any moment each one would break free and make a mad dash for the canyon's only exit.

Seven outlaws raced toward the corral with the intent of mounting horses and riding out. Two were picked off before they reached their destination. The other five made it safely to their mounts. To prevent the killing of any horses, the lawmen refrained from shooting at the five mounted outlaws in the corral.

Seeing that five of their comrades made it to their horses, a dozen more outlaws made a dash for the corral and their horses as well. Three were dropped in their tracks, but the other nine made it.

One frightened horse broke the top rail of the corral fence and jumped over the remaining two rails. Three more horses quickly took advantage of the broken rail.

The fourteen mounted outlaws followed the four frightened runaway horses out of the corral at a full gallop. In ten seconds, they would be at the mouth of the canyon. The only thing between them and freedom was Henry Watts and his six lawmen waiting at the exit.

Clint wasn't sure if he could hit a man on a running horse, but he was willing to try. He aimed his Winchester carefully and gently squeezed the trigger. A split second later, a heavyset man threw his hands skyward and toppled backward from his saddle, landing hard on the rocky ground.

Seven seconds later, gunfire could be heard at the mouth of the canyon. Six of the remaining thirteen mounted outlaws were cut down as they rode directly into the gun sites of Mr. Watts and his men. Unfortunately, seven outlaws made it through the blockade.

Mr. Watts promptly called down seven lawmen from their ridge-top positions; three from Captain O'Bryan's group, and four from Sheriff McDowell's group. He kept two of these men at his location and sent the other five in pursuit of the seven escapees. The five lawmen lit out on foot, running as fast as they were able to the arroyo where their horses were tethered. The seven escapees had a half-mile lead by the time the lawmen started their pursuit. Not even the two sentries that Mr. Watts had posted outside the canyon were able to stop the fleeing outlaws.

The two lawmen that Mr. Watts called down and kept at his key position were Chino Watson and Dewey Loomis.

After a ten-minute firefight, the canyon suddenly fell silent. For some strange reason, Kantrell signaled for his men to stop firing. The lawmen, puzzled once again by the unnatural action of wanted men, stopped their firing as well.

"Henry!" shouted the outlaw leader.

"What do you want, Kantrell?!"

"What ya say to let'n us ride out of here … and we leave Arizona for good?! We'll just mosey on down south to good ol' Mexico!"

Henry Watts didn't even need to think about Kantrell's offer. "No deal, Kantrell!" he replied.

"Now, *Henry*, I wish ya'd change yer mind!"

"I'm not changing anything! My answer remains the same—no deal!" Mr. Watts said with even more force.

During the exchange of words, seven more of Kantrell's men stealthily made their way safely to the corral. The horses that remained there were extremely nervous and huddled at the back of the corral. The seven men mounted up and made a break for it. Seconds later they were bearing down on Henry Watts and his reinforced location at the exit of the canyon.

Clint took aim at one of the fleeing riders and squeezed the trigger. His shot spattered the ground inches from his intended target. He was glad that he hadn't shot the fleeing man's horse.

Mr. Watts and his men opened fire. Five riders were

fatally hit and instantly toppled from their saddles. Another outlaw was catapulted forward from his saddle when his horse was shot out from under him. The one remaining rider in the group made it out of the canyon unscathed.

"Dadburnit!" Chino grumbled aloud. "I plum missed that mangy rider ... and now I've done gone and killed that poor ol' horse he was ridin'."

"Yeah, and that *hombre* that was ridin' 'im looks badly injured. He's tryin' to crawl over to that boulder," Dewey reported as he reloaded his carbine.

"I'll get him!" came the reply from a nearby deputy. "Cover me!"

That same deputy, who was standing behind Dewey and Chino, took off in the direction of the injured man in hopes of capturing him. He was about ten feet from his destination when a bullet cut him down. The shot originated from the injured man.

"We got a man down, Mr. Watts!" Dewey shouted out as he fired at the injured outlaw. "He ain't movin'!"

The injured outlaw that was catapulted from his horse managed to find cover behind a boulder.

"Mr. Watts!" Chino yelled. "Ya want I should go after that one feller that rode out of here?!"

"No, let him go! He's just one man. It's unrealistic to think we can capture them all. Maybe one of our sentries will take him down!" Mr. Watts replied.

On the left ridge of the canyon, two more lawmen fell prey to gunfire. Clint and his friends cringed when they saw them tumbling down the slope of the rocky ridge.

"Best I can tell, Jim," Clint began, "there's about thirteen of 'em left down there that ain't dead or wounded."

"I figured fifteen, but I like your number a lot better,"

Jim replied. "I think it's time we worked our way down this slope and see if we can capture a few of 'em."

"I'm ready whenever you are," Clint quickly responded. "How many men we got left on this side of the canyon?"

"Not countin' you and me—seven," Jim replied. "Chino and Dewey are down below with Watts."

"Geoff," Jim called out, "you stay here with the Domann brothers and Mike! I'm takin' Clint, Titus and Dave with me down to the canyon floor!"

"Okay, Cap'! We'll lay down some cover fire for ya!" shouted Geoff.

Jim, Clint, Dave and Titus started their descent. Geoff, Mike and the three brothers filled the air with cover fire. About twenty yards into their descent, Titus took a bullet squarely in the chest. He fell forward against a small boulder, slid over the top of it, and rolled down the side of the canyon.

"Oh, no! Tell me it ain't so!" Clint cried out. He wanted to rush to the aid of his fallen comrade, but the gunfire being directed at him made it impossible.

Down below, Russ Thorpe and two of his lackeys made a run for the corral. In mere seconds they were mounted and riding directly for the mouth of the canyon.

Henry Watts and his lawmen were waiting for them. The two lackeys were handily shot from their galloping steeds. Thorpe was wounded in his upper leg but kept on riding. As he sped through the blockade, he killed two of Mr. Watts' men. One of the dead was Dewey Loomis. He caught a bullet in the neck.

"Chino!" Mr. Watts bellowed. "Grab that dead man's horse over yonder and go after that low down *coyote!*"

Chino glanced momentarily at Dewey's lifeless body and took off in a flash. He launched himself into the

146

saddle in one swift movement and galloped dangerously at full speed down the narrow trail.

With two more lawmen dead and Chino in pursuit of Thorpe, Mr. Watts was left with only four men to protect the mouth of the canyon. It wasn't enough firepower to get the job done. More men would have to be called down from the ridges. He signaled for one man to come down from the right ridge and two from the left ridge.

Luke, the oldest of the three Domann brothers, quickly volunteered his services. He hurried down the right ridge and joined Mr. Watts and the two men from the left ridge. Mr. Watts now had a total of seven men at his strategic position.

Remaining on the left ridge were Sheriff Bob McDowell, Sheriff Tim Hayden, and two deputies. On the right ridge were Ranger Geoff Tingle, Marshal Mike Chandler and two of the Domann brothers—Matthew and John.

Six lawmen were now riding west in pursuit of nine escapees. One of the pursuers was Ranger Chino Watson. He was hot on the trail of Russ Thorpe—the man that had just killed his best friend.

Jim, Clint and Dave continued to make their way down to the canyon floor. Two outlaws were still shooting at them even though Geoff, Mike and the two remaining Domann brothers were still providing cover fire from the ridge above.

Suddenly, without warning, Clint saw movement out of the corner of his eye. He turned to his left and saw Two Scars rushing at him with his knife drawn. Clint had no time to aim and fire his Winchester or draw his single-action revolver. Instead, he jerked up his rifle to protect his body from the thrust of the knife. It worked, but the impact of Two Scars' body slamming against his body knocked him backward into a large boulder. The Winchester went flying out of his hand.

Two Scars slammed his body against Clint's body several more times in a life and death struggle. With all his might, Clint was pushing back the fisted right hand that held the razor-sharp knife. With his own right hand, he was beating on Two Scars' face. It was brute strength against brute strength. They struggled back and forth between the rocks for what seemed like an eternity to Clint. Neither had the slightest intent of giving in to the other.

It appeared that the struggle was favoring Two Scars until Clint managed to poke a finger into the aborigine's left eye socket. Two Scars, in extreme pain, reeled rearward just far enough for Clint to grab the Apache's right forearm with both hands and twist it around until he was able to plunge the knife blade deep into the renegade's sunburned flesh. The knife blade easily tore through the man's liver.

Two Scars' right hand fell limply to his side as he looked down at the knife sticking out of his abdomen. Clint, fearing retaliation, jerked the bloody knife out of the renegade's body. Two Scars winced. Hesitating for only a second, Clint plunged the knife into Two Scars' upper chest, fatally piercing his heart.

Two Scars' body jerked uncontrollably several times before he drew his last breath. He fell backward—crashing hard between two boulders—his life's blood oozing from his fatal wounds.

Clint extracted the knife summarily from the body of Two Scars, and wiped it clean on the Apache's buckskin pants. He would keep the knife as a reminder of how close he came to losing his life to the bloodthirsty renegade.

Butch Kantrell and his remaining eight uninjured

men made a dash for the corral. Two failed to arrive alive—thanks to the shooting accuracy of McDowell and Hayden. Kantrell and the other six made it to the corral and mounted up. As they were about to ride out, Captain Jim O'Bryan (who was now on the floor of the canyon) fired a shot at the outlaw leader—striking him in the left shoulder. The man toppled from his horse—wounded and dazed.

As the leader of the rangers was running up to him, Kantrell managed to fire a round from his old Navy .36 caliber revolver. The bullet struck Jim in the right forearm, knocking his Colt out of his hand. Kantrell, still dazed, clumsily eased back the hammer of his revolver to finish off his pursuer.

Dave Martin, who was standing near Jim, tried to fire off a shot at Kantrell, but the seven horses rushing at him made it impossible. He hastily leaped out of the way—barely avoiding the sharp hooves of the lead horse.

Jim, sensing he was done for, dropped to the ground just as Kantrell jerked the trigger. The bullet barely clipped the top of his right collarbone. Jim, with his ear only inches away, heard the whiz of the bullet.

Clint Wells, seeing Jim fall to the ground, rushed over to him to check on his condition. When he knelt down to examine his friend, he heard the double click of a hammer being pulled back. He turned quickly about and saw Kantrell aiming straight at him. Clint rolled to one side, jerked his Colt from its holster, and fired.

Kantrell, his eyes wild with rage, stared down at the large hole in his chest. His soiled white shirt was quickly turning red. He placed his left hand over the hole, looked up at Clint, then fell forward—dead.

The six riders that just escaped from the corral were now riding at a full gallop toward Mr. Watts and his reinforced position. There was a sudden hail of gunfire at the mouth of the canyon. One deputy was killed; however, none of the six outlaws escaped. All were brought down. Five were dead, and one was wounded.

The gunfire finally ended. An eerie silence fell over the canyon. The whole dreadful battle had lasted only thirty-five minutes, but it seemed like an eternity to all involved.

The four wounded outlaws, knowing that none of their comrades were alive—apart from those that escaped the canyon—threw down their weapons and surrendered.

The lawmen still remaining up on the ridges came down from their lofty positions. Minutes later, they were gathering around Henry Watts and the captured outlaws.

"Check them for hidden weapons ... and put some cuffs on them," Mr. Watts ordered.

One hundred yards away, near one of the lean-tos, Clint and Dave helped Jim to his feet. They assisted him to a nearby boulder and sat him down. He was wounded, but not critically.

"By the way, Clint," Dave began, "ya have been bleedin' from yer upper arm. There's a two-inch cut in yer shirt ... and a big ol' blood stain."

"Yeah, ol' Two Scars nicked me with his knife. It's not that bad. Just needs cleaned. I'm sure that knife of his had plenty of germs on it."

"I'll go back to the arroyo where we left our horses and fetch my first-aid kit out of my saddlebag," Dave said.

"That would be much 'preciated, Dave," Clint replied as he watched Dave turn about and scurry away.

Henry Watts sent a deputy back to fetch the horses *and* the four men guarding them. He didn't realize that Dave Martin was already headed in that direction. Had he known, he could have asked him to do it.

Luke promptly joined up with his brothers. They hugged each other in relief that they had all survived without a scratch. This was, to date, the biggest test of their courage since becoming lawmen. They would have one heck of a story to tell when they got back to Mesa City.

Henry Watts summoned Sheriff McDowell to his side. "Bob, where's our chief ranger, Captain O'Bryan?" he asked the most senior ranking sheriff.

"He's somewhere near the far end of the canyon. He's been shot. I haven't a clue how serious his wounds are," reported McDowell. "I saw him being helped to his feet."

"Well, thank goodness he's alive," replied Mr. Watts. "But we have lost some brave men here today. A total of seven, as best I can tell. Take what men we have standing here and collect the bodies of our fallen Heroes. We'll get a burial detail assembled as soon as possible."

"Yes, sir," McDowell said as he motioned for all, but one, of the remaining lawmen to follow him. He left one man behind to guard the prisoners.

Henry Watts suddenly felt like being alone. He walked over to a nearby rock outcropping and sat down. He felt sick to his stomach. The death of seven lawmen was not as bad as he had expected, but it didn't make it any easier to bear. And, he was also upset that Russ Thorpe and eight others had escaped. He wished now that he had posted more men at the mouth of canyon at the beginning of the battle. *It's my fault, and I'll take the blame for the tactical error,* he mumbled to himself.

A few minutes later, Mr. Watts stood up and walked deeper into the canyon in search of Captain O'Bryan.

At his earliest opportunity, Mr. Watts planned to make a full assessment of the raid. He needed to account for each lawmen and his present condition. He also needed to know for certain how many of the outlaws were dead, wounded, or on the lam. The governor would want a full and concise report.

Henry Watts' search for Captain O'Bryan was interrupted by the sound of many horses. He turned around to see six lawmen and a herd of horses bearing down on him. All the lawmen reined up in front of Mr. Watts—except for Dave Martin. Dave rode on past to where Captain O'Bryan was patiently awaiting medical attention.

Dave rode up to Jim and Clint and slid out of his saddle. He rushed over to his friends and presented the medical kit to Clint. Moments later, Jim's major forearm wound and minor shoulder wound were cleaned and bandaged.

"That wound above your collarbone is mostly a burn mark. It drew very little blood," Clint informed his friend. "However, your forearm will take a while to mend. Mesa City can't be too far from here. You can mosey over there tomorrow and have a *real* doctor take a look at you."

"Thanks, Clint—Dave. I'm glad the bullet went clean through my forearm without breakin' the bone," replied Jim.

"Yes, you were certainly fortunate," remarked Clint. "Someone was lookin' out for you."

"Allow me to clean and bandage yer cut, Clint," Dave said as he began to snip away the bloody, torn sleeve of Clint's shirt.

"By all means," Clint chirped, "have at it."

Dave wiped off the dried blood. "It's not deep. I'll have ya fixed up in no time," he reported.

When Dave finished with his doctoring, Clint called upon him for one additional task.

"Dave, can you help me fetch the body of Titus? He's lyin' over there near that large boulder."

"Certainly, Clint. Be glad to do that."

Clint and Dave walked off in the direction of their fallen comrade as Jim looked on. The three lawmen were not yet aware that they had lost Dewey Loomis, as well, in the battle for law and order.

Clint and Dave retrieved Titus' body and transported it to one of the lean-tos.

Clint, fighting back tears, cleared his throat. "He'll be out of the hot sun here."

"That's a good thing," Dave sighed. "Sir, would it be all right to use one of these bedrolls lyin' here to wrap up his body?"

"Certainly, Dave. Just make sure that it's the cleanest one you can find."

"Yes, sir, I'll look 'em all over very carefully."

Clint looked back to where Jim was sitting and saw him talking to Mr. Watts. He was glad that the governor's man was taking such an interest in the welfare of those who served here today. Clint knew that at least three lawmen had died in battle, for he had seen them fall. He prayed there were no others.

"Sir, this is the best of the bunch," Dave said as he offered up the blanket to Clint.

"It looks just fine, Dave. Let's get him properly covered."

Clint and Dave spread the blanket out, lifted Titus'

body up and placed it on one edge. Next, they respectfully rolled his body up in the blanket. Clint took the knife he had retrieved from Two Scars and cut away some of the hemp rope that was used to construct the lean-to. The rope was then used to bind the blanket securely about the young ranger.

"Reckon there ain't much more we can do for 'im," Dave surmised.

"No, I guess not," replied Clint, sighing heavily. "We'll get with Mr. Watts and see what his plans are as they relate to buryin' the deceased."

"Ya won't have to wait long—here he comes now," Dave said as he directed Clint's attention to the south. "Captain O'Bryan is with 'im."

"Ranger Wells," Mr. Watts began, "I'm so sorry for your loss. Jim told me how you took Ranger Green under your wing."

"Yes, sir, I reckon I did in a way."

"Mr. Watts," Dave said, "what are yer plans for buryin' our dead?"

"I've got Sheriff McDowell and the others gathering up the bodies of the other slain lawmen. We'll bury them outside of this canyon. I'm sure a proper location can be found that will be acceptable to all concerned."

"Clint," Jim began, "it's my guess that you're not aware that we lost *two* rangers today?"

"No, I had no idea," Clint responded, looking a bit ashen. He immediately thought of Geoff.

"Nor did I," echoed Dave. "Who was it?"

Jim, his heart heavy with grief, sadly replied, "Dewey Loomis was killed when he tried to stop Russ Thorpe from fleeing the canyon."

"I'm sorry to hear that, Jim," Clint answered. "I know he was a friend of yours."

"Is Chino all right?" Dave immediately asked.

"We don't know the status of Ranger Watson—yet," Mr. Watts said as he injected himself back into the conversation. "He's in pursuit of Russ Thorpe."

"What's the status of Ranger Tingle ... and Marshal Chandler?" Clint quickly inquired of the governor's envoy. "We left 'em up on the ridge to give us some cover fire."

Jim beat Mr. Watts to the answer. "They're all just fine, Clint. Not a scratch on 'em," he reported.

"Praise God!" exclaimed Clint.

Dave excused himself and went in search of Titus' horse. He planned to use the horse to transport the deceased ranger to wherever the burial site would be established.

"When you are done here, I would like for you all to join me at the mouth of the canyon. We'll have a short meeting and decide what to do with the bodies of our fallen Heroes ... *and* the dead outlaws," Mr. Watts concluded.

As Mr. Watts walked away, Jim sat down under the lean-to. He was feeling a bit wobbly.

"Hey, you feelin' okay?"

"Yeah, Clint. Guess I lost just enough blood to make me a bit dizzy. I'll be fine."

"Well, take it easy. No need to rush things."

"Here comes Dave with Titus' horse," noted Jim. "Sorry, but I'm not able to help you lift his body across the saddle."

"You just take it easy, Jim. Dave and I can manage just fine."

"By the way, my friend, how's *your* arm doing?" asked Jim.

"Oh, it's fine. Scars' knife barely nicked me."

Within a few minutes, the still body of Ranger Titus Green was loaded aboard his mare and secured. The town of Jerome would, at some future date, mourn its twenty-two-year-old fallen Hero. Rangers Wells, O'Bryan and Martin escorted their deceased comrade to the mouth of the canyon where Mr. Watts was assembling his troops for a meeting.

Chapter Eleven

It was three o'clock in the afternoon, and the lawmen were gathered around a campfire in Wild Burro Canyon eating a late lunch. The bodies of their seven fallen Heroes had long since been gathered up and buried on the summit of a small ridge just outside the entrance to the canyon.

The bodies of the outlaws were placed at the far end of the canyon. Their graves were shallow—like their lives had been—and covered only by enough stones to discourage critters from digging them up. There were thirty-two dead outlaws in all.

"I've got the final stats here if anyone is interested in hearing them," announced Mr. Watts.

"Yeah, I'd like to know how we did," replied Sheriff Tim Hayden.

"Well, gentlemen, on *our* side—seven deceased, two wounded, six still out chasing the escapees and, thankfully, twenty-two of us sitting here without a scratch on us."

Mr. Watts paused, wiped his brow, and then clarified a portion of his report.

"Uh," he began, "by saying *twenty-two*, I'm including the four men that were guarding our horses in the arroyo and the two sentries we had posted outside the canyon."

"What about *their* side?" Dave inquired.

"I'll bet it wasn't very good," remarked Luke.

"Well, *they* ended up with thirty-two killed—as those of you who were on the burial detail already know. I'm sure your backs feel broken about now."

"Don't remind me!" one of the deputies shouted out. He followed his comment with a weak chuckle.

"Sorry," Mr. Watts said with a smile.

"Continue with your report, sir," someone else shouted out.

"Yes, of course," Mr. Watts said as he cleared his throat. "Well, we've got four wounded outlaws shackled over there by that boulder, along with two of their sentries that our uncover agents roughed up a bit and took into custody.

"And, unfortunately, we have *nine* outlaws on the lam—including Russ Thorpe. The good news is, Thorpe is wounded. That ought to slow him down."

"Ranger Chino Watson is pursuin' 'im, sir," Jim began, "and I can guarantee you that he *will* get his man."

"I hope you are right," Mr. Watts said.

"You must keep in mind, sir, that Ranger Loomis was Chino's best friend. He will avenge his death even at risk to his own life," explained Jim.

At that moment riders could be heard approaching. It was the five deputies that had ridden out in pursuit of the first seven escapees. They rode up to the campfire and dismounted.

"Glad to have you back, men," Mr. Watts said as he

rose to his feet to greet them. "Did you succeed in stopping any of them?"

One of the Phoenix deputies, Coulter Rayburn, readily offered up his report.

"As ya know, we went after seven men. We caught up to 'em 'bout six miles from here. They were headed north on the stage road. Some gunfire was exchanged. We got three of 'em, sir. The other four gave us the slip."

"That's not a problem," Mr. Watts said, smiling. "You did the best you could. I'm sure those four will not slow down until they get to Utah—or anywhere else but Arizona."

Ranger Tingle was quick to speak up. "Mr. Watts," he began, "there was one lone outlaw that rode out of here shortly after the first seven made their escape. Have we a man on *his* trail?"

"Well," Mr. Watts began as he rubbed his chin in contemplation, "I reckon we don't."

"We didn't see any outlaws but the seven we went after," Deputy Rayburn added to his report. "An' we was keepin' a sharp eye peeled."

"So," Sheriff McDowell began, "in summary, we have Ranger Watson in hot pursuit of Thorpe, four that eluded Deputy Rayburn and presumably heading north to Utah, and one lone escapee heading for who-knows-where with no one on his trail."

"That's how I read it, too," Sheriff Hayden said.

"Ya want I should take a couple of men and go back out and look for that one lone escapee, Mr. Watts?" asked Deputy Rayburn.

"No, Deputy, that's not necessary. You've done enough for one day. It's time to rest and eat. Come on over to the campfire, men, and fill your plates with some beans and jerky. I wish I had something much more appetizing to offer you."

Henry Watts didn't consider it a tragedy that only one outlaw got away without ever being pursued—or that four others eluded his deputies. Those were numbers he could live with.

Mike leaned over and tapped Clint on the shoulder. "Those other four outlaws are headed north—straight for Payson," he whispered. "My gut tells me that the citizens of Payson will be in great peril when those outlaws hit town. I've got to head for home as soon as possible."

"Yes, you're absolutely right. I hope that new deputy you hired will be able to handle things until *we* get there," Clint replied in a low voice.

"I hope so, too," echoed Dave. "I'd hate for anything to happen to Sarah. I'll be tag'n along, too."

"I 'preciate ya both wantin' to help. Thanks," Mike replied.

Clint patted his friend on the shoulder. "No problem. I'm glad I'm able to help out."

For the next few minutes only the sounds of the desert could be heard—the gathering call of Gambel quail being the most predominant sound. Not far away, a Cactus Wren was singing its song.

Captain O'Bryan finished his meal, set his plate on the ground, and turned to his friends. "I'm worried about Chino."

"Yeah, so am I," echoed Dave. "I hope he's on his way back to us."

"Should I ride out and look for 'im?" asked Geoff. "I don't mind at all."

"No, that wouldn't help. But thanks for offering," Jim responded. "Maybe he'll show up soon."

"He might be waitin' for us at our campsite over by Sycamore Creek—thinkin' we'll show up there sooner or later," suggested Dave.

"Yeah, we'll hope for that," Jim said.

Henry Watts stood up, waved his hand for attention, and made a final announcement. "Gentlemen, as soon as you've eaten your fill and are ready to travel—we'll ride out of here. I don't want to linger here too much longer," he said.

Everyone was in total agreement.

* * * * *

Chino Watson could not figure out why Russ Thorpe chose the route he did. Instead of staying on the stage road to Mesa City, he veered off to the east after crossing the Rio Salado.

Chino surmised that Thorpe was either heading for the Goldfield Mountains or the Usery Mountains. Neither mountain range would offer up an effortless path of escape.

It had not been too difficult tracking the outlaw. For one, his horse had lost a shoe; and secondly, all Chino had to do was follow the drops of blood. Based on the number of drops, Chino was betting he would find his man dead before the day was out.

By two o'clock, the ranger had tracked his man for nearly twelve miles. It now appeared that Thorpe was headed for the Usery Mountains.

Chino was nearing the base of the small mountain range when he saw the horse. It was deceased. Its hide was soaked in foamy lather. The flies had already discovered the carcass. Nearby were more blood droplets.

They led up a well-worn path in the direction of the tallest peak. From his vantage point, Chino could see what looked like a cave near the top.

Still in the saddle, Chino set out on the narrow trail. After climbing roughly two hundred feet above the desert floor below, he reached a point where a horse could not easily go. He dismounted, tied the horse to a nearby Palo Verde, and began climbing on foot. He soon found that frequent rests were required. He wished he had some water to drink.

The blood droplets were increasing. How Thorpe could keep going with such a loss of blood confounded the ranger. *The man ought to be dead by now,* he mumbled aloud.

After climbing a few hundred feet more, Chino could see the cave clearly. It wasn't so much a cave as it was a deep hollow in the mountain carved out most likely by the wind.

As he came to within fifty yards of the wind cave, a shot rang out. Chino could feel and hear the bullet speed past his left ear. He ducked for cover.

The ranger did not know how much ammunition his adversary had on him. He hoped not much. Chino made a quick count of his own supply of bullets. His pistol contained five unspent cartridges. There were nine pistol cartridges still stored in the loops of his holster belt. The carbine he held in his hand had about six cartridges left in it—if his memory served him right. He now wished that his revolver and carbine used the same caliber of shell. Sadly, they didn't.

"Thorpe!" Chino yelled out.

"Wha-what ya want, lawman?!"

"Ya need to come on down from there! Ya are gonna bleed to death if ya don't git to a doctor real soon!"

"I-I'd rather ble-bleed to death than ha-hang!"

Thorpe fired another shot at the ranger. His aim was getting worse. The bullet missed Chino by a foot or more.

I'm guessin' he's git'n weaker by the minute, Chino thought.

Chino began climbing again—ducking from boulder to boulder. He gained another twenty feet in elevation. From his new vantage point, he could see Thorpe. The man was leaning against the back of the wind cave.

The ranger leveled his carbine, took aim, and fired. The bullet struck the cave wall inches from Thorpe's head and ricocheted away. Tiny shards of rock struck Thorpe in the cheek. He did not move.

Chino didn't know if his man was dead or playing possum in an effort to lure him in for the kill. *There's only one way to know for certain*, he mumbled, *I gotta go up there and find out.*

Chino left his cover and headed straight up the trail. When he got within thirty feet of Thorpe, he pulled his revolver from its holster and aimed it directly at the outlaw. He fired at the man's foot. The bullet struck the heel of the outlaw's boot. He didn't move. Thorpe had bled to death.

Kneeling at the outlaw's side, Chino collected the man's revolver and holster. He didn't see a carbine anywhere in the area, and so he assumed that the outlaw never had one from the start of the chase.

Dealing with the outlaw's body was Chino's next concern. It was obvious that this wind cave was a popular destination for the locals. There were human signs everywhere. One such sign was a ring of rocks around a hole that was dug in the hard earth—a fire pit.

Chino decided to haul the body back down the mountain as far as he was able. He tied his carbine to the backside of his belt. Next, he lifted Thorpe's body up and across his shoulders. For the next twenty minutes, he struggled hard to get the body back down the mountain. But realization soon set in, he did not have the strength to continue.

The ranger left the trail and traveled about twenty yards to the west. He found what he was looking for, a secluded spot behind a large boulder. He placed the body down and covered it with many large stones. The task was exhausting.

The seasoned ranger rested for nearly thirty minutes before starting back down the mountain. His best friend, Dewey, was finally avenged.

Chino retrieved his borrowed horse and headed for the rangers' campsite at Sycamore Creek.

* * * * *

It was late in the afternoon when the lawmen and Henry Watts arrived at the Sycamore Creek campsite. They were all glad to be back in familiar surroundings.

Clint was concerned with the wound in Jim's forearm, and expressed his concern to Mr. Watts.

"Worry not, Ranger Wells," replied Mr. Watts. "It just so happens that one of my staff members is a trained medical assistant. I thought it prudent to bring him along on this campaign. He will take good care of your captain."

"I'm certainly glad you were thinkin' ahead. It will save us a trip to Mesa City," Clint replied. "I'll go fetch my boss and bring him over to your tent."

"We'll be waiting for you."

Clint hustled to his campsite and fetched Jim from his tent. He informed his long-time friend about the medic. It made his day.

"I don't remember anyone sayin' we had a medic among us," Jim commented.

"Neither do I—but I'm not gonna fuss about it."

A professional was soon patching up Jim's arm. The medic had all the necessary bandages and antiseptics needed to properly treat the wound. The most painful part of the procedure was when he cauterized the wound to stop it from oozing blood.

Clint escorted Jim back to their campsite.

"I'll bet that hot iron against your skin hurt plenty?" Clint supposed. "I'm glad it wasn't me on the receiving end of it."

"Boy, did it ever," Jim admitted. "I think it hurt more than the bullet did."

As soon as they arrived back at their campsite, Clint prepared a campfire so he could make coffee.

"I'm goin' huntin'," Dave Martin announced.

"Huntin'? Huntin' for what?" Clint asked.

"I saw some jackrabbits as we were ridin' back in here. I think I can git us some fresh meat to eat."

"Hey, I'm all for that," Geoff said. "Ya better hurry though, it's gonna be dark in a couple of hours ... an' ya barely got half uh moon for light."

"Ya mind if I join ya?" Mike Chandler asked.

"Not at all. The more the merrier," Dave replied.

"Are we walkin' or ridin'?" Mike asked.

"Walkin', of course!" Dave exclaimed.

"Wish I had my shotgun," Mike said.

"Yer carbine will work just fine on 'em long-eared

jacks," Dave replied. "Just aim for their head," he respectfully instructed his friend.

"I'm wantin' the shotgun for shootin' quail," explained Mike, clarifying his previous statement.

"Oh, I see," said Dave. "I ain't never before ate me any of 'em ol' quail. Are they any good?"

"I love the taste of fresh quail," Mike said. "The breast meat is white—like a chicken's breast."

"I've eaten dove," Dave replied. "That meat is the color of a chicken's liver."

"Too wild tastin' for me," commented Mike.

"If ya soak the meat overnight in salt water it'll remove the wild game taste," replied Dave, in an effort to instruct his friend on proper preparation of dove. "Makes a world of difference in the taste."

"Ya don't say. Maybe I'll try that someday."

Moments later, the coffee was ready. Clint poured a cup for himself, Jim and Geoff. Then, he sat down and joined them in conversation. Clint informed his friends that when he got home, he was submitting a letter of resignation. It didn't matter whether the rangers were disbanded or not.

"Now, hold on a minute, Clint," Jim began, "you don't want to do that."

"And why not, pray tell?"

"Stay with the rangers until the end of the year. If we are disbanded, the governor is fixin' to dole out severance pay to all those on the active *and* reserve payroll roster. You'll certainly qualify."

"Where did ya hear that, Cap'?" asked Geoff, with a grunt. Earlier he had been critical that the rangers were getting the "boot" without so much as a pat on the back from anyone.

"From Major Tom Williamson. He has *informed* connections among the political elite in Phoenix. They leaked the information to 'im," Jim explained.

Clint said, "Hmmm, perhaps I'll wait after all."

Suddenly, a rifle shot could be heard, followed by a second. It startled Geoff.

"A bit jumpy, huh, Geoff?" Jim remarked.

"After today—ya bet I am," countered Geoff.

"It sounds like our big game hunters hit on somethin'," Clint remarked.

"I hope it's tasty," Geoff said with a grin.

Fifteen minutes later, Mike and Dave strolled into camp carrying two field-dressed jackrabbits. They held them high for all the rangers to see. The only thing left to do was run a stick through them and roast them over an open fire. The rabbits would be a nice change from all the beans, jerked beef and hard tack they had eaten the past few days.

"Already cleaned," Clint said. "I'm impressed."

"We shot 'em—so y'all can cook 'em," Mike quipped as he offered the jackrabbits to Clint.

"Be glad to do that," Clint responded as he reached out and took possession of them.

* * * * *

It was nearly dark by the time Chino rode into camp. He was dog-tired.

He asked immediately if his mare and Dewey's gelding had been brought back from Four Peaks. He was pleased to learn that both horses were tethered with the rest of the mounts.

"I've pretty much killed that mare I've been ridin' all

day. She's 'bout done for," Chino said, with sadness in his voice. "A horse should not be used up like that."

"What about Russ Thorpe?" Jim asked.

"He's dead. Bled to death. Tracked 'im all the way to the Usery Mountains. Found 'im in a wind cave. He shot at me a couple o' times before he died. I buried 'im up there on that mountain," Chino said as he concluded his report and sat down.

"We're glad you're back with us," Jim said.

"Where did y'all lay Dewey to rest?" Chino asked.

"Him and Titus are buried at the base of Four Peaks—just outside the confines of that canyon," Clint replied. "We even put up some wooden crosses."

"I'm gonna miss ol' Dewey. He was a darn good and faithful friend to me," attested Chino.

"I have no doubt," Jim said sympathetically.

"If'n ya don't mind, Captain, I'd like to keep that gelding ol' Dewey rode," Chino requested. "It's a real fine horse—much better than my own."

"I'm sure Dewey would have wanted you to have his horse," Jim replied.

"Yeah, I'd like to think that's the case."

"You can have his holster and pistol as well," Jim added.

"Thanks, Captain."

"Chino, are ya hungry?" Mike asked. "We've got a few pieces of rabbit left."

"Bring it on! I'm so hungry, I could eat it raw!"

"No need to do that," Dave said with a chuckle.

The five rangers, along with Marshal Mike Chandler, sat around the campfire talking well into the evening. They were glad that their mission was nearly over.

Hopefully, Mr. Watts would release them from duty in the morning.

Captain Jim O'Bryan took a moment to thank everyone on his team for supporting him. He expressed his sincere desire that the rangers stay in touch with each other after the territorial government disbanded them.

Ranger Chino Watson entertained the group with a few "war stories" concerning his friend, Dewey, and how they came to be such good friends.

Rangers Geoff Tingle and Dave Martin told a few tales of their own.

Marshal Mike Chandler expressed deep concern about the four outlaws that were headed north toward Payson. He was more than anxious to depart for home in the morning—and said as much.

Captain Clint Wells eulogized Ranger Titus Green, and then adjourned the gathering with a word of prayer— thanking God for bringing them out of a dangerous situation all in one piece.

"Amen," Jim said.

* * * * *

Many miles to the northeast, Connie was getting her stepdaughter, Lena, ready for bed. Assisting her was her step-niece, Maree.

"You seem a little stressed today, Aunt Connie."

"Yes, I suppose I am. According to Captain O'Bryan's itinerary, today was the likely day that the lawmen were to go up against the outlaws. I'm just overly concerned about Clint and his friends."

"I understand," Maree said as she picked up Lena and carried her off to her bed. "I'm sure they will be just fine."

169

"I know it's in God's hands. I guess my worrying isn't going to change anything, huh?" Connie said as she followed Maree and Lena into the bedroom.

Maree placed Lena in her bed and gave her a kiss. "I would not argue that point."

Connie gave Lena a kiss and placed a blanket over her. "Goodnight my little angel."

Maree and Connie adjourned to the kitchen.

"I'm so glad you are spending the night, Maree. I wasn't looking forward to another evening alone."

"Well, I must confess—I had another motive."

"Oh? Would you like to share?"

"Aunt Connie, I think, I'm in love with Chip."

Connie was taken aback by the revelation. "You're serious—aren't you?"

"Yes, ma'am, I am. And I need some grownup advice," Maree confessed. "So, what do I do now?"

"Does Chip know how you feel?"

"No, ma'am. And I don't know how to tell him."

"I'll make some coffee—then, we'll talk," Connie said with a smile.

Chapter Twelve

Tuesday, October 13th.

As usual, Clint was up at the crack of dawn. He was sitting on a nearby boulder reading the Scriptures when Jim interrupted him.

"Sorry for the intrusion, Clint," he began, "but would you be interested in trek'n over to Mesa City and spendin' a day or two for some rest and recuperation?"

"Well, I certainly would like to see the place, Jim. But I reckon git'n home to Connie and Lena is a lot more important to me than a day of rest.

"And, there's a second good reason—I promised Mike that I would ride back with him to see if those four fugitives stopped in Payson for a little R 'n R of their own. He's worried himself to a frazzle about that possible situation."

"I kinda figured you'd want to get home right away. Can't fault you one bit. Reckon if I had a family and a ranch to run I'd be hightailin' it home too. Us ol' single types don't have too many responsibilities outside of our job and our horse."

"Perhaps one day you'll have a wife … and lots of kids, too."

"Yeah, perhaps. Anyway, reckon me and Chino and Geoff will ride over to Mesa City as soon as we are released from duty here. We need to unwind somethin' terrible."

"Well, y'all certainly earned a little time off," Clint replied.

Jim chuckled. "I hope to tell you we did."

"I guess you know that Dave is all set to go back to Payson with Mike and me?"

"Yeah, I heard. He's mighty anxious to get back there and see that cute little waitress, Sarah. I see wed'n bells in that boy's future.

"And, as for Mike, it's like you said, he's anxious to get back, too. He's got that *greenhorn* deputy, Kip Jones, handlin' things … and I know for a fact that it worries 'im a good deal."

Jim turned and started to walk away.

"Hey, Jim!"

Jim stopped and turned about to see what Clint wanted.

"While you're in Mesa City, my friend, stop at the doc's office and have that arm looked at again."

"I'll do that," Jim promised. "Reckon I'll get some coffee to brewin'. You want some?"

Clint nodded his head and returned to his reading. But he was unable to focus. His mind kept drifting away to his family and his ranch. He missed his wife and daughter intensely, and he just wanted to get home. Besides that, he went off and left a twenty-year-old wrangler in charge of the place.

Mesa City can wait, Clint thought. *I'll go there with Connie and Lena some day.*

* * * * *

It was a chilly, but beautiful morning at the Rim Shadow Ranch. Chip Bowman was up before six o'clock. He liked to get as much done as possible before breakfast.

So far, he had been keeping up with the chores around the horse ranch, and he hoped that his boss, Clint Wells, would notice his efforts when he returned from duty at Four Peaks.

Dusty Rhodes had been filling in for Clint at the Double Creek Ranch. Chip was pleased that the stagecoach duty was not one of his many obligations.

By seven o'clock, Connie Wells was up, dressed, and preparing breakfast for herself, Maree, Lena and Chip. She was nursing a cup of strong, black coffee as she flipped over the bacon that was sizzling in the big iron skillet. Just like her husband, she preferred her bacon extra crispy.

And, her husband was more on her mind than her cooking. She hoped and prayed that he was all right, and that he would be coming home today, or tomorrow at the very latest.

Her thoughts were interrupted by a knock at the door. It was Chip. He had arrived for breakfast.

"Come in, Chip!"

Chip entered and sat down at the kitchen table. He leaned over and tickled Lena under her chin. The little girl giggled and tried to tickle him back.

"Ma'am, is Mr. Wells comin' home today?"

"Oh, I do hope so, Chip. I don't think I can endure another day without him."

From the back of the house, Maree suddenly appeared. Chip immediately stood up. She flashed her eyes at him as she sat down at the table. "Good morning, Chip," she said, demurely.

"A fine mornin' to you, too, Miss Maree," the wrangler said as he sat back down at the table. He couldn't believe that he was fortunate enough to be sitting at the same table with her.

"Chip, can we talk later?" she asked. "It's rather important."

"Sh-shore. We c-can do that," he stammered.

* * * * *

It wasn't too long before the rangers and Marshal Mike Chandler gathered around the campfire for coffee and fried potatoes.

"I shore could eat a mess o' fried eggs and bacon," Dave said. "I'll be headed for the Yellow Sun Café the first chance I git."

"Eggs? Bacon? Ha! Ya will be headed over there to see Sarah ... an' ya know it," teased Geoff.

"Well, maybe that's a lot closer to the truth," confessed Dave, a grin forming on his face.

"When are we ridin' out, Jim?" Clint asked.

"Mr. Watts wants us all together for a meeting in about forty-five minutes," Jim replied. "After that, I'd say we are free to go our merry way."

"Captain, do ya want any of that horse feed my packhorse is tote'n before we split up?" Mike asked.

"Naw. I'll get what horse feed I need in Mesa City," Jim answered.

There was silence for a brief moment.

"Oh, Mike," Jim blurted out, "I almost forgot—since that government-owned packhorse that I brought along has to go back with me—we'll need to transfer Dave's belongings to your packhorse. Is that all right with you?"

"Certainly," Mike said. "My packhorse is travelin' light now that more'n half of the feedbags are empty."

"Clint, would you like to have Titus' pup tent?" Jim asked. "It's a fairly new one."

Clint nodded his head. "That would be nice."

"I think Titus would have wanted you to have it," Jim added. "Thanks to your witness, Titus is dwellin' in a very lovely place right about now ... and it's far better than some ol' tent."

"Praise the Lord," Clint replied. "I thank God each and every new day for His love and forgiveness and mercy. Where would we be without Him?"

"Let me guess," Jim began, "at a place hotter than the desert in the middle of July."

Everyone chuckled at Jim's assessment.

"What ya gonna do with Titus' horse?" Mike asked. "It's a nice lookin' mare."

"When Titus joined the rangers, his own horse was not up to standards, so the government purchased that mare for 'im to ride," explained Jim. "I've got to turn her in when I get back to Fort Verde. She'll probably be sold or loaned to someone else."

"What happened to his six-shooter and holster?" asked Geoff, only out of curiosity.

"Since his holster and six-shooter were not in very good shape, we left 'em on him when we wrapped him in that blanket. They're buried with his body," explained Clint.

Jim had the final word on the subject. "As for his bridle and saddle, reckon I'll check and see if he has any relatives around Fort Verde that might want to lay claim to 'em," he said.

* * * * *

Following breakfast at the Rim Shadow Ranch, Maree followed Chip to the barn to assist him with the preparation of Connie's buggy.

"How do ya like workin' at the café?" he asked.

"I like it very much," she said enthusiastically. "Connie is training me to become a chef."

"Hmmm, I'll have to come over there one day and try out some of yer vittles," he said as he attached the rigging to the horse.

"Oh, that would be grand!" she said excitedly.

"Ya wouldn't mind?" he asked.

"No, not at all," she quickly said. "It'd be my pleasure to cook for you—anytime."

There was a long pause in the conversation as Chip finished hooking the horse up to the buggy.

"I'm done," he announced. "Let's git this buggy over to the house."

"You sure can do that fast," she said. "I guess you get a lot of practice."

"Yep, six mornings a week!" he answered.

There was another long, uncomfortable pause in their conversation.

"Miss Maree, ya said ya had somethin' ya wanted to talk 'bout," he reminded her as he backed the horse and buggy out of the barn.

Maree's heart was pounding. "Chip ..."

"Y-yes?" he said, feeling rather nervous.

"Chip, I'm very *fond* of you. And I—"

"Ya are?" he interrupted. "That's wonderful—'cause I feel the same 'bout ya, Miss Maree."

"You do? Really?" she said, shocked by the revelation. "I had no idea, Chip. This is grand news!"

Both Maree and Chip felt as though a great suffocating weight had been lifted from their hearts.

"What do we do now?" she asked.

"Does Mr. Wells or Mrs. Wells know how ya feel 'bout me?" he asked as he bit down on his lower lip.

"Aunt Connie knows. She encouraged me last night to talk to you … and tell you how I feel."

"Thank you, Mrs. Wells!" he blurted out. "Ya must tell yer uncle soon. We'll need his approval."

"Yes, I know. I'll do that the next time I see him— which could be in the next day or two."

Chip tied the horse to a corner post that supported the corral and motioned for Maree to follow him back inside the barn. She complied.

"What is it?" she asked when they were out of view of the house and any possible prying eyes.

"J-just this," he said as he took her into his trembling arms and planted a long, passionate kiss on her warm, supple lips.

Maree thought she would pass out. Her head got woozy and her heart rate soared. By the time Chip released her, her knees started to buckle.

He caught her in the nick of time.

Chapter Thirteen

Captain O'Bryan and his small group of lawmen finished their morning meal, then began to break camp. Within thirty minutes, they were ready to travel.

"Well, fellers, let's join the others at the main tent and see what Watts has to say," Jim said. "I hope his speech won't take too long. I know some of you are itchin' to get on the road."

"I'm certainly ready to hightail it out of here," Mike said as he looped the strap of his canteen over the horn of his saddle.

"And that goes for me, too," Dave commented.

The final meeting took place at the main tent as scheduled. Henry Watts thanked everyone for their outstanding service. He promised that all those involved would be getting a special citation from the governor. He said wanted posters would be issued for the five outlaws that escaped the canyon. Lastly, he went around and shook every hand before dismissing all the lawmen.

"I like that man," Clint commented. "Wouldn't surprise me none if he ended up run'n for governor some day."

"Yeah, he's an all-right fellow," Jim agreed.

"I'll give 'im two thumbs up," Dave said.

Chino and Geoff nodded in agreement, but didn't say anything. Their thoughts were focused on getting as far away from Four Peaks as was possible.

"I guess this is where I say 'goodbye' to y'all," Jim said, addressing Clint, Mike and Dave. "I hope y'all have a safe trip back to Payson."

"Thanks, Jim. I'm sure we will," Clint replied. "And, Jim, keep in mind that my ranch is always open to you. Come by anytime for a visit … and stay as long as you like. I might even put you to work."

"I'll be sure to do that," Jim promised. "Perhaps as early as next spring."

"Be lookin' for you to show up."

"I'll give you plenty of advance notice before I come. I don't want your wife git'n peeved at me. Some women don't take too kindly to unexpected company."

"That'll be fine, Jim," Clint said.

Clint, Mike and Dave said their 'goodbyes' to Jim, Geoff and Chino. Everyone shook hands before mounting their horses and riding out. Apache seemed aware that he was going home. The black stallion began to dance around and shake his head. For a brief moment, Clint thought he might rare up.

At the stage road, Clint, Mike and Dave turned north; Jim, Geoff and Chino turned south for Mesa City. The trip to Mesa City would take about three hours or less, but the trip to Payson was closer to two days.

"*¡Adios, mi amigos!*" Clint yelled out when the two groups were about a quarter-mile apart.

The southbound group turned in their saddles and waved.

Soon the two groups were out of sight of each other.

Mike grunted. "If we didn't have this packhorse, I'll bet we could make it home tonight."

"I'd hate to put that much stress on my colt though," Clint replied. "Besides, it wouldn't do your critter any good either."

"Yeah, ya got a point there," Mike agreed. "I guess I'm just overly worried 'bout things in Payson."

"I understand," Clint said. "Reckon I've been worried just as much about things at the ranch."

No one said much for the next mile. Mike was the first to finally break the silence.

"Say, Dave, will ya be goin' on to Fort Verde on Thursday—after yer visit with Sarah Benson?"

"No, sir. I figure Captain O'Bryan won't be back at headquarters until Saturday or Sunday, so I'll spend a couple of days in Payson. If he can take a couple of days off—well, so can I."

"I'm sure Miss Sarah will like that very much," Clint commented. "She certainly seems like a nice young lady."

"Yes, sir, I couldn't agree more with yer assessment," Dave said. "She's the sweetest gal I ever met. It's gonna be real tuff ridin' back to Fort Verde without her."

"If she's *the one*—God will make things happen for you," Clint commented. "Don't ever leave Him out of the picture."

"I hear what ya are sayin'—but it shore ain't easy bein' patient sometimes."

Clint chuckled. "You can say that again!"

The three lawmen rode all day, stopping only when necessary to rest and water their horses and grab a bite of food for themselves. By late afternoon, they had reached their old campsite located just north of the second way station.

"What do ya make of that, Clint?" Mike asked.

"Well, pard, it looks like someone has been campin' here. The coals are still smolderin'. I'd say whoever built this fire left here about three or four hours ago."

"Except for the stagecoach, we didn't meet anyone on the road goin' south, so whoever it is—they are travelin' north just ahead of us," Dave surmised.

Clint nodded. "I'd say you're right on target. And, by the tracks they left behind, I'd say three—maybe four—horses."

"Ya don't think it could be ..."

Mike stopped mid-sentence as he carefully studied the tracks.

Clint read his mind. "Not sure, Mike," he answered as he dismounted. "You just never know. It may well be our escapees from Wild Burro Canyon."

The lawmen busied themselves by getting the horses unsaddled and rubbed down, and freeing the packhorse of its burden.

"Dave, if you'll do some huntin' for us, Mike and I will set up the campsite," offered Clint.

"It's a deal!" Dave said as he retrieved his carbine from his scabbard and went marching off into the high chaparral.

Barely thirty minutes had expired from the time Dave left camp until a gunshot could be heard in the distance. Not long after that, Dave walked into camp showing off his fresh, field-dressed kill.

"Fresh meat two nights in a row!" Mike exclaimed. "It doesn't get any better than that."

"Well, I can't wait to eat some *real* meat," Clint complained. "I'm talkin' about a big, juicy steak!"

Everyone got a laugh out of Clint's remark. They would have preferred a steak to rabbit as well.

"I guess Jim, Geoff and Chino are havin' a good time in Mesa City right 'bout now?" Dave surmised. "And, I'll bet money they ain't chewin' on rabbit."

"I hope Jim got that arm looked after when he got to the city," Clint said with much concern.

"It looked like it was healin' pretty well," Mike said. "That medic at Watts' tent looked at it again before Jim rode out of camp this mornin'."

"That's good," Clint said. "Reckon I should've had him take a gander at this cut on my arm. It feels okay, but you just can't be too careful with a knife wound."

"I'll fetch my first-aid kit, Clint, and clean it up for ya," Dave offered.

"That's mighty kind of you, Dave."

It wasn't long before Clint's knife wound was washed and wrapped with fresh bandages. It looked like it was healing nicely.

"Clint, we got us a good doctor in Payson," Mike remarked. "It'd be a smart move to have him look it over at the first opportunity."

"I'll do just that," Clint replied with a nod.

Several minutes went by without anyone speaking. Each man was preoccupied with his private thoughts. Clint was thinking of his family, Mike's thoughts were on his duties in Payson, and Dave was thinking about Sarah Benson.

Dave was the first to break the silence. "Mike," he began, "do ya think there's any chance another deputy position will open up soon at yer office?"

"Well, I don't rightly know, Dave," Mike replied. "I suppose a position might become available sometime in the not-so-distant future. As you know, Payson is growin' at a pretty fast pace. I'm guessin' we'll probably need more'n one deputy before long."

"What if that new deputy ya got now wasn't meetin' yer expectations?" asked Dave, fishing for a solution to his need.

"Then I'd say a job would be open real soon."

Mike paused for a brief moment. He knew exactly where the conversation was heading. He decided to get to the point.

"Dave, are ya applyin' for a job?" he asked.

"Yes, I am! But I can't start until after the first of the year. That's when the rangers go extinct."

"Yeah, I heard that was happenin' to y'all. I think it's a big mistake. Don't ya think so, Clint?"

"Yes, I do. But I can understand where the governor is coming from. I think, he realizes that the various sheriff departments throughout the territory are growin' in numbers and doin' a better job than ever before at enforcin' the laws.

"I think, too, that the two departments were git'n annoyed at each other over who should be in charge of a case. The sheriffs want more say in how things are done."

"Reckon I can see where that would cause some disputes," Mike replied. "I just hope they don't decide to do away with us town marshals."

184

"I wouldn't worry none about that Mike," replied Clint, hoping to soothe his friend's worry.

"Dave," Mike began, "if somethin' opens up, ya will be the first person on my hire list. Ya realize, of course, that the town ain't gonna pay ya what ya make now?"

"Yeah, I kinda figured on that bein' the case," Dave sighed. "But I like Payson. It's a far better place to live than Fort Verde. And, I like the people."

"Of course you do, Dave. One citizen in particular," teased Clint. "Now, what was that gal's name? It keeps slip'n from my memory."

"Ya are *soooo* right," Dave admitted. "And it's Sarah—as though ya didn't know."

"I knew that," Clint said. "I'm just messin' with you, pard."

The lawmen ended their fireside conversation and prepared to call it a day. Soon, they were in their bedrolls and fast asleep. They decided not to take turns at guard duty. Hopefully, they would not regret their decision.

* * * * *

Several miles to the north, at a way station in a beautiful box canyon near Rye Creek, four weary men were preparing to hunker down for the night. They had no bedrolls or blankets. They would be sleeping on the bare floor inside the station house—at the expressed displeasure of the station manager.

Their bed *this* night would be better than the bed they had the previous night when the hard, stony ground was their bed, and the seats of their saddles were their pillows. For warmth, they used their numnahs (sheepskin saddle pads) as blankets.

185

The reason for their predicament was simple: they rode out of Wild Burro Canyon the previous day with barely more than the shirt on their back. These men were some of the last survivors of Kantrell's gang of outlaws.

When they fled the canyon they were a gang of seven, but the lawmen pursuing them had gotten the best of them. Over a six-mile stretch, the lawmen—exhibiting outstanding marksmanship—had managed to whittle down their number to four.

Thanks only to young, able-bodied horses, these four managed to outrun their pursuers. Their goal now was to get to Payson, steal some money and supplies, and beat a path for Utah or Nevada. It didn't matter which.

One of the men extinguished the lantern that was illuminating the front room of the way station and slowly made his way to where the others were sacked out on the floor.

"Hey, Jack, do ya think there's much money in that ol' Payson bank?" Andy asked as he tried in vain to make himself comfortable. He was a tall, thin man, not more than thirty years old. He had been rustling cattle since he was nineteen. As yet, he had not killed anyone.

"It don't matter much. We got nothin' now—so even a hundred dollars is a lot of money," Jack replied, sourly. He was a heavy-set man, roughly forty years old. Killing came natural to him. He got a thrill out of carving notches in the wooden grips of his six-shooter. Presently, there were fifteen such notches.

"I just wish we had some decent food to eat," complained Bucky, the youngest of the four. He was probably twenty years old. Even he wasn't sure of his age. He had never learned to read or write, and some would say that he was even a bit slow of mind. He was a killer, but unlike Jack, he didn't take any pleasure in it.

These men had raided the cupboards at the way station, but found little to satisfy their palette.

"Oh well, I reckon we'll have all the food we need when we git to Payson," Bucky chirped. "Even if we gotta steal it."

"We do gotta *steal* it, ya moron!" Jack quipped. "'Cause we got no money!"

"Don't be callin' me that!" Bucky warned.

"Hey! Go to sleep ya two," Lefty ordered. Since he was the oldest, he envisioned himself as the leader of this small band. He was in his mid-fifties, of average height and weight, and was nearly bald. He was an experienced bank robber, and had killed when it suited him.

"Who put ya in charge?" Jack snapped.

Lefty grumbled. "Hey, didn't we do enough fightin' yesterday? We don't need to be fightin' 'mong ourselves."

"He started it!" Bucky countered.

Jack apologized. "Okay! I'm sorry, Bucky."

* * * * *

Connie had just put Lena to bed when she heard a knock at the door. She went to the door to investigate. It was her brother, Robert.

"Robert!" Connie said in a surprised tone. "What in heaven's name are you doing over here after dark? Is everything all right? Is Aunt Helen all right?"

"Oh, yes. I didn't mean to frighten you by calling this late. I didn't make it over today to check on Chip, so I thought I'd best look in on y'all."

"We're fine. Just missing Clint, that's all. And getting somewhat worried," she confessed.

"Sis, why did you ask about Aunt Helen?"

"She wasn't feeling good earlier today while working at the store. I suggested to her that she should stay home tomorrow and rest."

"Hmmm, she's fine now as far as I know. But, I'll check on her when I get back to the ranch. If anything is wrong—I'll hustle back over here and let you know."

"That would be greatly appreciated. She doesn't go to bed for at least another hour. She ought to be up reading about now—unless she's worn out."

"Well, come to think of it, I did see light emanating from her bedroom window."

Robert quickly changed the subject matter from Aunt Helen to his brother-in-law. "This is Clint's fifth night away from home, right?" Robert asked with concern.

"Yes, but it seems like five months. I do hope and pray he's on his way back."

"Well, I'm sure if there had been any problems you would have gotten word by now," he said in an effort to ease her anxiety—and perhaps his own.

Not wanting to dwell on her husband's absence—as it depressed her greatly—Connie changed the subject again. "Robert, would you like something to eat or drink?" she asked. "I wouldn't mind fixing you something."

"No, no. It's too late for that. I'm just glad you are doing okay. Is there anything I can do for you around here tomorrow? I'll have a few hours free in the afternoon."

"I can't think of anything. Chip is doing a fine job. I'm proud of him ... and Clint will be, too, when he finds out how well the young man has kept the place up-and-running like a well-greased wagon wheel."

"Yes, that's true. I came over a couple of times to help him ... and he worked circles around me.

"Clint certainly knows how to judge a man's character.

He finds good people in the same way he finds good horses.

"You know what they say: 'You *are* who you hang out with.' And Clint's friends are some of the nicest people I know," he concluded.

"Well, there is *one* exception, Robert."

"Oh? And just what is that *one* exception?" he curiously asked.

"He hangs out with *you*, big brother," Connie teased, while grinning broadly as she patted him on the arm.

"All right, Sis, that's enough of that. Now give me a hug so I can be on my way."

Connie hugged her brother and bade him farewell. Robert, with lantern in hand, headed for the path leading through the woods to his ranch. She watched him from the porch until he disappeared from her sight.

Connie went to Lena's room and checked on her one more time before heading to her own bedroom. All was fine.

Now in her own bedroom, she stared at the big empty bed and greatly wished that her husband didn't have to be away. She longed to feel his body next to hers, to feel his lips pressing against hers, and to feel his hands caressing her body.

She sighed deeply as she slipped off her clothes and swiftly donned her near ankle-length cotton nightgown. She pulled back the quilt and slid between the soft flannel sheets. For the next several minutes she simply focused on the blank ceiling above. Finally, she leaned over and blew out the candle that was sitting on the nightstand. It was going to be another long and dreary night without her man to comfort her.

Lord, please bring him home soon, she prayed, and then she closed her eyes.

Chapter Fourteen

Wednesday, October 14th.

Clint Wells, like so many other mornings, rolled out of his bedroll at the first hint of daylight.

Before heading out to complete his morning ritual, he tended to the campfire. And, before rousting Mike Chandler and Dave Martin out of their slumber, he made certain that the coffee was brewing.

Thirty minutes had lapsed by the time he walked over and shook the tent poles. In a not too loud voice he shouted, "Come on, you two, get up … and greet the new day!"

"Yes, *mother*," moaned Dave.

"Say, ranger, ya shore can be bossy early in the mornin'," complained Mike, somewhat sourly.

"No doubt in *my* mind," Dave agreed. "Ya'd think he was promoted to captain or somethin'."

"Come to think of it, Dave, he was," Mike said with a chuckle.

"Sorry, but I'd like to ride out of here in the next hour—if that suits y'all?" Clint remarked.

"I can readily agree to that," replied Mike, followed by a big yawn. "The quicker I get to Payson and find out what's goin' on—the better I'll feel."

Each lawman drank his fill of black coffee and ate several warmed up biscuits before preparing his horse for travel. Clint prepared the packhorse.

"Make sure that campfire is out, Dave," cautioned Clint. "We certainly don't want to spoil the beauty of this place with a wildfire. It's kinda nice just the way it is."

The lawmen broke camp around eight o'clock. Their next stop was the way station located in the scenic box canyon near Rye Creek. There they would find a fresh-water well from which to fill their canteens and water their horses.

Two hours later, they rode up to the secluded way station. The station manager, seeing their badges from his kitchen window, came rushing out onto the porch to greet them.

"Ya are too late! They're gone!" he shouted.

"Who's gone?" Clint asked.

"Those four *coyotes* that ya are lookin' fer—that's who!" he said, his voice readily reflecting his irate mood. "They spent the night here—over my heated objection."

"How long ago did they pull out of here?" Mike asked as he dismounted.

"I reckon it ain't been more'n an hour," the angry manager reported.

"Good. That means they won't arrive in Payson that much ahead of us," Mike declared.

Clint and Dave dismounted. As each ranger was about

to tie his horse to the hitching rail, Mike reached out and took the reins from them. Along with his own horse, and the packhorse, he led all the animals to the water tank.

"Thanks, Mike," Clint said. Then he turned his attention back to the station manager.

"Did they harm you in any way?" Clint asked.

"They gave me this here black eye when I tried to run 'em off. But mostly, they just got under my skin," he replied. "Ate what little food I had, too. They were just like a bunch of no-account skunks—git'n into everything."

"We have some extra canned goods that you are more'n welcome to," Clint replied. "We are only goin' as far as Payson."

"I heard 'em talkin' 'bout Payson. Said they was gonna rob the bank there."

"We'll be waterin' our horses and fillin' our canteens before we ride out. I hope that's okay with you?" Clint said.

"Help yerselves, rangers. Take what ya need."

"Dave, would you fetch some canned goods from the packsaddle and give 'em to Mr. ..."

"Hardin, is my handle!" the station manager quickly volunteered. "Pete Hardin—down from Montana way."

"To Mr. Hardin," Clint said, finishing his sentence. "I'm Captain Wells—this is Ranger Martin—and over by the water tank is Marshal Chandler from Payson."

Dave took notice that Clint was now identifying himself as a captain. *I think Clint is ready to accept his title,* he thought.

"Glad to make yer 'quaintances!" Pete Hardin said with a grin forming gingerly on his sore, bruised face. "An' I hope ya lock up them stinkin' *varmints* that was here stealin' me blind."

"We'll do our best, sir," Clint replied.

Fifteen minutes later, the lawmen were back on the main road and heading north at a slow trot.

"I'm not shore how much damage those four *yahoos* can do before we catch up to 'em—but I'm hopin' no one gets hurt if they try to rob the bank," Mike said with concern flashing across his face.

"The horses aren't that tired, so maybe we can lope 'em along for a couple of miles," suggested Clint. "The terrain is mostly flat here."

"Let's do it!" Mike concurred.

By noon, they were just a dozen or so miles south of Payson, and climbing in elevation at a more pronounced rate. The landscape before them was gradually changing with each additional mile. Some cedar scrub was now visible on both sides of the road. It had a very distinct aroma.

Two miles later, they came across a rather disturbing sight. It was another smoldering campfire.

"That has got to be our fugitives," Mike guessed. "They took a breather here."

"Evidently, our fugitives don't have enough common sense to put out their campfire," Clint said, sourly. "Dave, would you ..."

Dave removed his canteen from his saddle horn and dismounted. "Got it covered, Captain," he said as he ground-tied his horse and walked to the campfire.

"Use all the water you need to drown it out, Dave. We've got plenty," Mike said. "A pile of dirt and rocks over it ought to finish the job just fine."

A few minutes later, the lawmen were back on the

dusty roadway and maintaining a steady pace. Mike prayed that they were closing the distance between themselves and the outlaws.

A few miles later, Mike let out a war whoop. "Rangers, there's our first stand of ponderosa pine!" he exclaimed. "It won't be too long now."

"Thank goodness," Dave muttered aloud.

Sensing that the horses were becoming rather fatigued, the lawmen had to rein back on their forward pace. It was better to arrive late, than not at all.

* * * * *

From a low ridge on the southern edge of town, four men were scanning the main street of Payson for signs of activity.

"We'll split up here so as not to bring attention to ourselves," Lefty said.

"Sounds reasonable," said Jack.

"I'll ride in first with Andy," continued Lefty. "We'll tie up in front of the bank.

"Jack, ya will ride in next and position yerself near the marshal's office.

"Bucky, ya are to ride in last. I want ya to tie up outside the saloon."

"Then what?" Bucky asked.

"Andy and I will enter the bank while ya two watch the street for any lawman that might show up and try to spoil our plans," explained Lefty. "If either one of ya see a tin badge—shoot first and ask questions later. Ya both got that?"

"Yep," grunted Jack. "That works for me."

"We gonna ride out after that?" Bucky asked.

"No, we ain't. We is gonna git us some food and blankets and whatever else we need for our trip."

"And a couple o' bottles o' whiskey—right?" inquired Andy, hoping for a positive reply.

"Ya bet we are! The best they got in that saloon," Lefty responded. "Yes, sir—the best they got."

"What are we uh waitin' for?" Jack spouted. "Let's go!"

"Wait here at least ten minutes before ya ride in behind us," Lefty ordered. "Any questions?"

"Nope," Jack said.

Lefty glanced over at Andy. "Okay, Andy—let's ride!"

Lefty and Andy were soon out of sight. Jack was sitting askew in his saddle trying to take some of the pressure off his tailbone. Bucky dismounted and began to bend his knees to relieve the stiffness in his legs.

"Do ya think Lefty's plan will work, Jack?"

"Shore, Bucky, why wouldn't it?"

"I don't know, Jack. Reckon I just got this strange feelin' in my gut."

"It'll be fine, Bucky."

"I wonder how many tin badges they got workin' down in that ol' town?"

"It don't matter none, Bucky. There's four of us ... and they ain't expectin' trouble," Jack said as he straightened himself in the saddle. "It will go as smooth as ice on a frozen pond."

"Yeah, I guess maybe it will at that."

Several minutes passed without any additional conversation. Then suddenly the silence was broken.

"Mount up, Bucky. It's time to ride."

Bucky grabbed the saddle horn and hastily swung

his body into the saddle. His sudden action caused his horse to panic and swing its rump around in a counter-clockwise arc just as his tailbone landed hard in the saddle. Bucky struggled with his mount for a brief moment before getting his right foot planted firmly in the stirrup. Soon he was in control of his horse.

"I'm ready, Jack," he breathed with relief. "Let's do it!"

Chapter Fifteen

The lawmen were about a mile south of Payson when they heard gunfire. They counted seven shots in all.

"Sounds like serious trouble in town!" Mike exclaimed as he stiffened his body and prepared to spur his horse into action. "I've got to hurry in there!"

"No, hold on a minute, Mike!" Clint said as he grabbed Mike's rein. "Cool heads must prevail. I think we need to ride to the south edge of town, leave our horses in a safe place, and walk in carefully."

"Ya are right, Clint. Sorry. I just lost my head," Mike said as he settled back in his saddle and took a deep breath.

Clint leaned over in his saddle and handed the pack-horse's lead rope to Dave. "Dave, take control of the pack-horse. Mike and I are gonna ride on ahead. Catch up to us as quickly as you can. Stay clear of the main street when you arrive in town. Hide the horses behind one of the stores ... and be ready for possible gunplay," Clint instructed.

Dave nodded his head. "See ya in a bit."

"Okay, Mike, let's get after 'em!" Clint ordered.

In a matter of seconds, Clint and Mike were gone in a cloud of dust. Dave could only go as fast as the packhorse allowed—which wasn't much more than a steady lope.

At the south limits of the small town, Clint and Mike reined in their mounts, dismounted, and secured the horses behind an out-building.

"Mike, let's cut through the pines to the backside of the barbershop," suggested Clint.

Arriving at the barbershop, they eased between it and the adjacent building. Stealthily, they reached the board-walk that paralleled the main street. They carefully surveyed the broad street in both directions. Except for a few horses, the street was empty.

"This can't be good," Mike observed.

"We'll split up. I'll check out the bank—you try to get to your office and see where that deputy is," Clint instructed. "If you see somethin'—whistle."

Clint had his Winchester rifle poised for action. Mike jerked his Colt from its holster. Clint headed west; Mike went east.

Mike had ventured less than twenty yards when he saw someone lying in the dusty street near his office. He got closer. It was his deputy, Kip Jones. He was not moving.

Mike knelt down on one knee beside his slain deputy before whistling for Clint to join him. A minute later, Clint's eyes were gazing down upon the same grotesque scene. "Is he dead?" Clint asked.

"Yeah," Mike answered, his heart heavy with grief. "This is cold-blooded. His gun is still holstered. I wish I knew where them *vipers* were hidin'."

Because the street was wholly void of citizens, Clint

was reasonably certain that the outlaws were still in town and lurking about in one of the surrounding buildings. He tapped Mike on the shoulder and directed him to check the mercantile store.

"They might be stockin' up on supplies," Clint whispered. "I'm headin' back to the bank."

Clint raced across the street, then made his way stealthily along the boardwalk in the direction of the bank. Once there, he peeked in the window and saw a body lying on the floor. At the far end of the room he espied a teller tied up near an open safe. No one else was visible to him.

Clint slipped past the big window and eased the door open. No one was in the room but the dead man and the teller. Clint rushed over to the teller and pulled the gag from his mouth.

"Are you all right?"

"Yes, sir. The manager is tied up in his office. As soon as you get me loose, I'll go free him."

"Who's that over there on the floor?"

"Just an innocent customer who wouldn't give up his money. He had just withdrawn two hundred dollars and was walkin' out when them two *skunks* come bustin' in the door with guns at the ready."

"You said *two* men—I'm thinkin' there should have been four of 'em."

"I don't know about that—only saw two."

"How much did they get out of the safe?"

"Not more'n five thousand," the clerk surmised. "They put it all in one bag. Thankfully, we got a hidden safe where we keep the bigger amounts of cash and gold."

Clint untied the teller, examined the man on the floor, and rushed back outside. When he got to the hitching rail, he spotted Mike waving his hand and pointing toward the saloon. Clint acknowledged his signal and carefully made his way to Mike's location.

"What's up?" Clint asked as he tried to catch his breath.

"The storekeeper said he saw all four of 'em go into the saloon. He said the man wearin' the checkered vest killed my deputy."

As Clint and Mike were cautiously making their way to the saloon, Dave stepped out of the alley near the barbershop. Spotting his friends, he promptly caught up to them.

Speaking in a hushed voice, Dave asked, "Where are they, Captain?"

"We believe they're in the saloon," Clint replied in a near whisper. "You slip around and come in through the back door. Mike and I will come in the front. Stay out of sight, remain quiet, and cover our play."

"Give me a minute or two to git myself in position," Dave requested in a low voice.

"Remember, stay out of sight. I don't want 'em to know that you are behind 'em," Clint whispered as they reached the front, outside corner of the saloon.

Clint motioned for Mike to come closer. Clint peaked in the window and saw two men at the bar with guns drawn. One had on a checkered vest. Two more were standing near a card table. The four patrons at the table were being picked clean of their valuables.

It was time for the lawmen to make their play.

"They've got their backs to us," Mike whispered.

"Yeah, that gives us a slight advantage," Clint whispered. "They'll have to turn about to shoot."

"How do ya wanna handle this?" Mike asked.

"Mike," Clint whispered, "the two standin' at the bar

are yours. It appears that one of 'em is wearin' a *checkered vest.*"

Mike nodded as he eased back the hammer on his revolver. "Yeah, I noticed."

As quietly as possible, Clint and Mike eased up to the front entry of the saloon. Clint positioned himself to the left; Mike took the right. Clint signaled to Mike that he was ready to move forward.

Clint and Mike burst through the bat-wing doors at the same time. Clint focused on the two men at the card table; Mike's focus was on the two outlaws at the bar.

"Drop your guns! Hands in the air!" Clint bellowed out at the top of his lungs.

The bartender, rightly sensing gunplay, quickly ducked behind the counter. The men sitting at the card table immediately spilled out of their chairs and crawled on hands and knees across the wooden floor seeking cover. All scampered to nearby tables and hid beneath them, with their hands covering their heads.

Jerking their heads around and seeing two determined men with shiny badges pinned to the front of their vests, and weapons at the ready, was all the outlaws needed to spur them into action. They spun around on their heels and leveled their pistols at the two lawmen.

Nothing short of evil showed in the faces of the four wanted men. Evil curses spewed from their mouths as they prepared to fire their weapons.

Almost instantaneously, five different pistols and one Winchester .44-.40 rifle discharged. The noise was nothing short of deafening.

The loud roar of the gunfire could be heard all up and down the main street. Several townsfolk braved a peek from the store windows, and a few even spilled out onto the boardwalk for a possible glimpse of the gun battle. But not one single citizen dared to go near the saloon.

Down the street, at the local church, an elderly preacher was praying for the safety of the lawmen. Earlier, he had witnessed the killing of Kip Jones as the unsuspecting deputy walked out of his office—directly into an ambush. The preacher was almost certain that the deputy never saw the outlaw that snuffed out his life with two close-range shots.

At the Yellow Sun Café, Betsy Lovemore had ushered her patrons safely out the back door. She was now armed with a shotgun. Sarah Benson and another young wait-ress were hiding out in the café's storage locker.

Sarah was aware that Marshal Chandler had returned to town—for she had seen him across the street, only mo-ments ago, checking on the welfare of his deputy. However, she wasn't certain that Dave Martin was in town—for she had not seen him. Nevertheless, she was praying that he was not on the receiving end of the hot lead that was fly-ing about in the saloon.

And the heavy lead bullets were indeed spewing dan-gerously about in the saloon.

Ranger Martin, who was stealthily lurking in the sa-loon's storeroom, jerked his pistol from its leather holster and moved forward toward the open door that led to the barroom. He could see the smoke filling the large room and smell the pungent gunpowder. He was eager to join the fray, but Captain Wells had told him to remain out of sight in the storeroom and block any escape attempt.

More shots were fired. Dave quickly slipped back into the shadows of the storeroom and waited to see what would transpire next.

He didn't have to wait long.

Chapter Sixteen

Clint and Mike fired their weapons in unison. Two of the outlaws were instantly hit—one standing at the card table and another at the long mahogany bar. Neither outlaw got off an accurate shot. One man's bullet punched a hole in the floor, while the other man's bullet plowed into the wall high above the heads of the lawmen.

The man who was struck at the card table crashed down on top of the table—breaking off two of the table's legs. He, then, spilled onto the floor—the table flipping on top of him. The man at the bar (wearing the checkered vest) grabbed at his chest, spun around, and crumpled to the floor—knocking over a spittoon.

The remaining two outlaws managed to get off one shot each. One man's bullet slammed into the door-frame just inches from Mike's shoulder. The other man's bullet tore at Clint's left shirtsleeve, but missed tearing his flesh.

Like a jack-in-the-box, the bartender appeared suddenly from behind the bar with a sawed-off, double-barreled shotgun at the ready. He pointed the muzzle of the shotgun at the outlaw nearest him and pulled the trigger. The blast knocked the startled outlaw sideways several feet, and nearly cut him in half. He immediately dropped to the floor—his life's blood pouring out faster than a slaughtered hog.

The last surviving outlaw ran for the back door, firing a hopeful second shot at the two lawmen as he fled. The bullet struck Mike in his left hip, causing him to crumple to the floor in agonizing pain.

Dave was waiting in the shadows for the fleeing outlaw. "Freeze—or I'll drop ya where ya stand!"

Realizing that he was hopelessly trapped, the outlaw tossed aside his revolver and surrendered. Dave immediately took him into custody.

"Mike, are you hurt bad?" Clint asked his friend as he stooped down to help him.

"The bullet only creased me," Mike reported. "Give me a hand up, Clint."

Mike slowly got to his feet and looked about the room. "What a mess! Is everyone all right?"

The bartender was the first to speak.

"Yeah, I guess. It's for certain we're doin' better now that you and your ranger friends are here."

The saloon patrons that were lying on the floor nodded their heads as they got back on their feet. Then one of them hastily made his way to the nearest dead outlaw and began retrieving his property from the man's pockets. His friends quickly joined him.

Just like a bunch of buzzards swoopin' down on a fresh kill, Clint thought.

"Marshal, where in blazes did you find them rangers?" asked the bartender.

"We were workin' together on a campaign down near Four Peaks. We've been gone several days."

"I think they killed that new deputy of yours."

"Yeah, I saw 'im lyin' in the street. I've got to hustle back out there and see to 'im."

"There's more bad news, Mike. A customer has been killed over at the bank, too," Clint sadly reported. "An elderly man."

"Any idea as to who that man might be?"

"I didn't get his name. The teller only said that one of these men struggled with the customer before killin' him ... and that he pried two hundred dollars from his tightly curled fingers."

"Marshal, I just found a wad of bills in this man's vest pocket," one of the card players announced.

"Bring it over here so I can count it," Mike ordered. "I'll take it back to the bank later. They can deposit it back in the customer's account. If he has a wife, she can do what she needs to do with it."

"It'll most likely be used for a down payment on his funeral," the bartender quipped.

Mike counted out the money. It came to two hundred dollars. "Yep, this is it," he declared as he put the money in his shirt pocket.

"Gotta get back to Kip," Mike said as he departed the saloon—limping as he walked out.

"There's a bag here somewhere with the bank's money in it," Clint said to Dave. "Do you see it?"

"Here it is, Captain!" Dave shouted as he leaned down near the overturned spittoon and picked up the bag. He walked across the room and handed the bag to Clint.

Clint went over to the broken card table and instructed one of the patrons to summon the undertaker. The man went straightaway to his assigned destination.

"Dave, go ahead and take your prisoner over to the

city jail," Clint ordered, "and see if you can coax some information out of him."

"Yes, sir. I'll be more'n glad to do that."

Dave pushed the outlaw ahead of him through the bat-wing doors. Clint stayed behind a moment longer to give the remaining saloon patrons some instructions.

"Y'all finish collectin' your property from these *ya-hoos*, but don't you dare take what don't belong to you. Am I bein' clear enough?" Clint said. "I'll be collectin' their guns and other possessions later."

Mike was in the street checking on his deputy. Several townsfolk had now gathered around. The local doctor came rushing up. He checked for signs of life. There was none to be found. The doctor looked at Mike and shook his head.

Mike turned to the doctor and said, "Doc, there's another gunshot victim at the bank."

"I'll go check it out," the doctor said as he stood up and rushed off in the direction of the bank.

With a heavy heart, Mike asked the men standing about him to carry the deputy's body to the undertaker's place of business. They immediately complied.

Clint departed the saloon and walked over to the bank. As he was about to reach for the door handle, the doctor opened the door and stepped out.

"Doc, what's his condition?"

"He requires an undertaker—not a sawbones," the doctor reported. "Sorry."

Clint entered the bank. The first thing he noticed was a blanket covering the body of the unfortunate customer. Clint stepped around the body and approached the teller's cage.

"Ranger, is it safe out there?" the teller asked.

"Yeah. All's fine. I just need to return this money. I reckon it's all here. Do I give it to you?"

"Wait here, I'll go get the bank manager."

A moment later the manager appeared and introduced himself to Clint.

"It was simply ghastly. We've never been robbed before now," the bank manager testified as he dabbed at his forehead with a handkerchief to remove the highly visible perspiration.

"And I hope it will be the last time you're robbed," Clint commented.

"My teller said that you've recovered all the money. My depositors will be happy about that."

"Yes, sir. I think you'll find it's all here," Clint said as he surrendered the overstuffed moneybag to the bank manager. "I just need a receipt."

"Not a problem," the manager said.

"The money taken from your slain customer was recovered, too," Clint added. "Marshal Chandler will be drop'n it off later."

"That's very good news. His widow will certainly appreciate that. They didn't have much money."

For the next ten minutes, Clint gleaned details about the robbery from the bank manager and teller. He even acquired the name of the slain customer. It would be noted in his report.

From the bank, Clint went directly to the marshal's office. By the time he arrived, Dave had already completed his interrogation of the prisoner.

"Did you find out his name, Dave?"

"Yes, sir, I did. His name is Andy Hart. Claims he was born in Kansas. He came to Arizona with his older brother lookin' for adventure." Dave took a breath. "I reckon his adventure will soon come to a neck-breakin' conclusion at the end of a hangman's new rope."

Clint nodded. "I'd say you're right."

"He claims that his pal, Lefty Moore, killed that customer at the bank."

"I doubt seriously that it will make much difference to a jury as to who killed the bank customer. He took part in the crime ... and he's just as culpable in my book."

"I just hope the judge and jury agree with ya."

"Did you say his last name was *Hart*?"

"Yes, sir."

"I came up against an outlaw at my ranch two years ago by the name of Hart. He was tryin' to steal a horse. I wonder if he's some relation?"

"Let's ask 'im."

Clint and Dave walked to the cellblock and peered through the iron bars at the captured fugitive. He was sitting on the edge of the lower bunk bed. He appeared a bit tense. Seeing Clint, he stood up.

"I've been informed that your name is Hart ... and that you have an older brother," Clint said.

"*Had* an older brother!" he replied, his words spewing forth in a vindictive manner.

"What happened to 'im?" Dave asked.

"Got hisself killed awhile back—by some sharpshootin' woman while tryin' to *borrow* a horse."

"What was his first name?" Clint asked, feeling edgy and somewhat queasy in his stomach.

"Aikey—Aikey Hart! And what's it to ya?"

Clint turned pale and suddenly felt sick. *What are the odds of arrestin' the brother of the man that had a part in the killin' of my first wife?* he inwardly asked himself.

"Captain, are ya all right?" Dave asked.

"Can't say as I am. I need some fresh air," Clint said as he headed for the front door with Dave in close pursuit.

Clint sat down on a nearby bench. Dave joined him. "Sir, is that outlaw we got locked up in there a brother to the man that killed yer first wife, Lisa?"

"Yes, Dave, he is. Aikey didn't pull the trigger, his partner did, but he was just as guilty in my book."

"I'm so sorry that ya are havin' to relive that awful day."

"Yeah, me too," Clint said as he leaned forward and braced his forearms atop his knees. His head drooped. He let out a long sigh.

"Is there anything I can do for ya?"

"Oh, no. I'll be all right in a minute."

As he predicted, a minute later, Clint straightened up and leaned back. He removed his hat and wiped his brow with the sleeve of his shirt.

"Sir, he said that some *sharpshootin' woman* killed his brother. Was it Lisa that killed 'im?"

"No. She was already lyin' on the ground, slowly dyin' in my arms from a gunshot wound to the chest. There was another woman on the scene that terrible day. She had come to help me—with her carbine at the ready."

"May I ask who that woman was?"

"Yes, you may. It was Connie—my new wife."

"Whoa! Ya don't say."

"Yeah. She's one straight shooter—thank God."

Clint soon regained his full composure and went back into the office. He took a seat in a chair near the wood-stove. Dave filled the chair on the other side of the stove. "Dave, you've already mentioned Lefty Moore, so fill me in on the rest of your interrogation of our prisoner."

"Well, sir, the feller in the checkered vest—the one that killed the deputy—well, he was Jack Redstone."

211

"Hmmm, I've heard of him. He's wanted in Texas for killin' a cattleman and woundin' his wife. He was about as hard-hearted as they can get. It's good that he's finally out of circulation."

Dave nodded his approval.

"So who's the fourth one?" Clint asked.

"Reese Buckhannon. They called 'im Bucky."

"Don't know him—nor Lefty Moore, for that matter. We'll have to check out the wanted posters. I'm sure Mike has a drawer full of posters that we can sort through."

At that moment, Mike entered the office. He had been at the undertaker's office making arrangements for Kip Jones' funeral. He was visibly shaken. He limped over to his chair and sat down hard. He took off his hat and slung it across the room.

Dave looked over at Clint. Clint, jerking his head quickly to one side, motioned for his subordinate to step out of the office.

"Captain, I'll pack our horses over to the livery. I know they need feed and water somethin' bad," Dave said as he headed for the door.

"That's a good idea, Dave. Thanks," Clint replied.

Clint waited in silence for Mike to say something. He would wait the rest of the day if necessary.

A few minutes went by before Mike finally spoke. When he did, he poured out his grief over the loss of his deputy and the customer at the bank. He tried to blame the deaths on himself, but Clint would not allow him to do it.

"I should have been here. It was idiotic leavin' behind a *greenhorn* deputy to watch over things."

"Mike, you know darn well that I've been down that same awful path over Lisa's death. Trust me, friend, beatin' up on yourself is a no winner."

Clint and Mike talked for some twenty minutes. Slowly, Mike's mind-set took a turn for the better. Clint suggested that they go over to the doctor's office and have that gunshot wound looked at. Mike didn't hesitate to go. The pain in his hip was increasing.

While they were at the doctor's office, Clint excused himself so that he could check on Apache, who was now boarded at the livery stable—thanks to Dave Martin.

At the livery stable, Clint assured himself that his big black stallion was behaving, and that he was settled in for the night.

Dave had already seen to it that Mike's rented pack-horse and water bags had been returned to Jake, the stable manager. The unused sacks of feed were put back in storage for later use. The leftover canned goods were donated to Jake.

Seeing that Dave and Jake had properly taken care of everything, Clint decided to return to the doctor's office.

"Let's go check on Mike's progress," Clint said to Dave. "I left him over at the doc's office."

Clint turned and waved at the stable manager. "So long, Jake. I'll check back with you later."

Chapter Seventeen

Clint and Dave arrived at the doctor's office just as he was finishing up with Mike's hip injury.

"It's not bad at all," announced Dr. Toliver. "Even so, he'll be limping around for a few days."

"That's certainly great news," Clint replied.

"Clint, ya better have the doctor check yer knife wound before we leave here. Ya certainly don't need that cut git'n infected," Mike suggested.

"Yeah, good idea, Mike," Clint agreed.

"You got a knife wound?" asked Dr. Toliver.

"Reckon it's more like a scratch," Clint said.

"It's more'n a scratch, Doc," Dave countered. "He tangled with an ornery renegade Apache by the name of Two Scars," explained Dave, rather excitedly. "Sir, show 'im the knife ya took from ol' Scars."

Clint slid the knife out of its buckskin sheath and handed it to the doctor.

"You say this once belonged to Two Scars?" the doctor asked rhetorically as he rolled it about in his hand. "No wonder you kept it. It's a nice looking knife ... and has a good balance to it, too."

"I agree," Clint said as the doctor handed the knife back to Clint and reached for the antiseptic.

"This might sting a bit," the doctor warned as he pored some of the liquid on clean gauze and applied it to Clint's arm.

"Yeow! That smarts!"

Dave and Mike laughed aloud.

"All right, you two," Clint said, "cut me some slack."

"Ranger, I think you've been *cut* enough," Dr. Toliver said with a chuckle as he started wrapping the wound.

Clint grinned and nodded.

Five minutes later, Clint slipped down off the examination table. The doctor informed him that his knife wound was healing well, with no indication of an infection.

"Thanks, Doc." Clint said. "How much do I owe you?"

"No charge. You lawmen put your lives at risk for us folks today. We don't pay you near enough for your efforts. I figure this ol' town is in debt to y'all."

"Much 'preciated, Doc," Clint said as he shook the hand that had just treated him.

The lawmen walked from the exam room to the waiting room. As they were about to leave the building, Clint turned to his friends and asked, "Is anyone hungry besides me?"

"Do ya need to ask that?" Dave quipped.

"Yeah, I think I could eat somethin'," Mike replied as he patted his belly.

"I hope Sarah is on duty at the café," Dave said. "It would be nice to see her again."

"Uh, I got bad news for y'all. The good folks at the café ain't gonna let us in the front door lookin' and smellin' like we do right now," Clint said, chuckling. "I suggest we get ourselves cleaned up first."

"Good idea. I'm gonna ride out to my place, let my family know I'm home, then scrub up," Mike said.

"Reckon Dave and I will head for the barbershop," Clint said as he gently pushed Dave toward the exit door of the doctor's office.

As he followed them out the door, Mike said, "I'll meet ya in my office in roughly one hour."

"Okay, we'll see you then," agreed Clint.

En route to the barbershop, Clint and Dave made a brief stop at the mercantile store. Clint needed a new shirt and a pair of denims. The shirt that presently adorned his torso was badly soiled and had a bullet tear in the left sleeve. Two Scars had sliced up his only other shirt that he had brought on the trip. He had ceremoniously disposed of that bloody shirt in the previous night's campfire.

"I wish I had a new shirt," Dave commented.

"So grab one."

"Don't have the money to spare," Dave sadly admitted. "Payday ain't until next week."

"I'll spot you a couple of bucks. Can't have Sarah seein' my pard in a dirty shirt."

"Gee, thanks, Captain!" Dave said, smiling.

"No problem, my friend."

"Reckon we had best stop at the hotel sometime soon and secure a room," Dave suggested.

"Smart idea. We'll do that next."

Clint paid for the new clothes and departed for the hotel with Dave at his side. Minutes later, they had a room secured for the night. To show his appreciation for their brave efforts in saving the town from the four outlaws, the proprietor gave them a twenty percent discount on their room.

Clint and Dave finally made it to the barbershop. As they entered, the barber, Clifford Turley, greeted them with a warm smile. "Good afternoon, rangers. Welcome to my shop," he said. "And what can I do for you today?"

"I want the works—haircut, shampoo, shave and a hot bath," Clint replied. "How much will it cost me?"

"That comes to three dollars, sir."

"And I want the same for my sidekick here."

"Captain, I can't afford all that!"

"You can today, *mi amigo*. Call it—if you will—an early wed'n gift from me."

"A wed'n gift! Do ya *really* think that sweet gal will marry me?"

"Dave, I have no doubt whatsoever—providin', of course, you look nice and don't have the aroma of a sweaty horse."

Mr. Turley sent his helper, Elmer, into the back room to prepare the baths.

"Have you anyone here that can shine my boots and brush my hat?" Clint asked the barber.

"Yes, sir, I do. However, that will cost you an extra fifty cents."

"That's fine by me," Clint quickly replied.

"While you're in the bath, I'll have Elmer shine those boots for you ... and see to your hat."

Forty-five minutes later, Clint and Dave waltzed out of the barbershop—both looking quite dapper and no longer smelling like a pair of sweaty trail hands. Clint was simply amazed at the bright shine on his boots. He had given Elmer a four-bit tip for doing such a good job.

"Wow, I feel like a new man, Ranger Martin. The best four bucks I ever did spend. Now, I don't have to go home tomorrow to my wife lookin' like I was dragged in the dirt behind a plow horse."

"Sarah oughta like how I look, too. Thanks for everything ya did for me, Captain."

"My pleasure, Dave. Glad to help a man make points with his best girl. You'd do the same for me," Clint surmised as he twisted and adjusted at his new denims.

"What's wrong with yer pants, Captain?"

"I hate new denims," Clint complained. "They're so dang stiff. My legs will probably be raw by the time I get home."

"This new double-breasted shirt of mine is shore nice. It has a soft feel, too. I hope Sarah likes dark green."

"Dave, I'm shore she'll like any color you happen to wear."

Clint and Dave started walking toward the marshal's office. It had been over an hour since they last saw Mike.

"Let's hustle over to Mike's office and see if he's back yet," Clint suggested.

"Yeah, he's probably waitin' for us."

Mike was indeed waiting for them—patiently, of course. He was quick to comment on their new look when they entered his office. He said, "Wow, look at you two!"

"Ya like?" Dave asked.

"Gee whiz, Dave, that barber must have cut two pounds o' hair off yer head. Got to admit, ya look a sight better. But I'll draw the line at sayin' ya look handsome," Mike concluded with a laugh.

Clint laughed, too. "*Maybe* Miss Sarah will think he's handsome?"

"Thanks for the kind words, gents. I ain't had a haircut in nine months," Dave confessed. "I shore do feel a lot different—kinda naked like. Reckon I'll git used to it—in time."

"Got a package for ya, Clint. It came from Flag'," Mike said as he presented it to his friend.

Clint took the small box and opened it carefully. Inside were his shiny new captain bars. "Well, I'll be a ..."

"Here, let me and Dave have the honor of pin'n 'em on yer new shirt."

In short order, Clint was ceremoniously adorned with his new insignia of rank in the Arizona Rangers.

"Captain, I'd like to be the first to salute you," Dave said as he brought his right hand up to his right eyebrow.

Clint proudly returned the salute.

"Well, rangers, let's stop jawin' and hustle on over to the café and start chewin' on somethin'—like a big, juicy steak," Mike said.

"Ya don't have to tell me twice!" Clint exclaimed.

"Or me!" echoed Dave.

* * * * *

Mike Chandler's fertile mind was conjuring up a mischievous scheme as he walked to the café with his friends. When they reached the front door of the café, Mike paused just long enough to present his plan to Dave Martin.

"Dave, let's play a little trick on Sarah. Stay out here while Clint and I go in and sit down at a table in the back of the room. Sarah will no doubt wonder what's happened to ya. When she starts writin' down our order—ya come in quietly and slip up behind her."

"Ha! I can't wait to see how that turns out," Clint said.

"I'll do it!" Dave replied with a big grin.

Clint and Mike entered the café and walked to a table at the very back of the room. Sarah spotted them right away and quickly made her way to their table.

"Hello, Sarah," Mike said.

"Hello, Marshal. I'm glad you're back."

"So how have ya been, Sarah?" Mike asked.

"I've been worried sick, Marshal," she confessed. "I heard about the awful gunfight at the saloon. So, tell me, where's Dave?"

"Dave?" Mike said as his eyes went to Clint and then back to Sarah. "I'm not certain, Miss Sarah, that I know who are you talkin' 'bout."

"Marshal, you know darn well who I'm talking about. He was in here a few days ago—with you."

"Oh! *That* Dave! The same Dave that's standin' right behind you," Mike said as he struggled to suppress a snicker.

"Huh?" Sarah uttered as she pivoted about on her heels.

"Hi, honey!" Dave said. "Did ya miss me?"

Sarah let out a sharp squeal. "Oh my goodness! You're here at last. I-I've been ..."

She never finished her sentence. She flung her arms tightly around Dave's neck and gave him a kiss so hot with passion that it would have melted butter in ten seconds or less.

Over by the checkout counter, Betsy Lovemore, the owner of the café, started clapping her hands. Almost immediately, every customer in the café was applauding. Clint and Mike promptly joined the celebration putting their hands together, too.

Sarah hastily stepped back and began to blush. Dave was about as red-faced as his girlfriend. Needless to say, neither was sorry for the public display of affection.

"Sit down, Dave," Clint ordered. "Love's great, but you need some food to sustain life, too."

Sarah quickly composed herself, adjusted her skirt, and took their orders. She disappeared in a flash. A moment later she was back with their coffee. Betsy Lovemore, owner of the café, was with her.

"Glad to have you boys back ... and in one piece," Betsy said. "I heard about the gunplay at the saloon. Ghastly affair. Also heard, Mike, that you took some lead in the hip. Are you doing all right?"

"Reckon I'll be sore for a few days. Doc says that I should recover just fine."

"Good," Betsy replied. "Oh, by the way, gentlemen, your meals are on me tonight. You earned them."

"That's very nice of you! Thank you, ma'am," Clint said, in a sweet, appreciative tone.

Mike and Dave hastily echoed Clint's appreciation with thanks of their own.

"You are welcome. Enjoy your dinner, gents," she said as she departed for the kitchen.

Sarah appeared again, this time at a nearby table. Her hands were noticeably shaking as she was taking the new patron's order. Clint glanced over at Dave and noticed that his eyes were following Sarah's every move.

"So, what's run'n through your mind, Dave?" Clint asked. "You look as though you're in a trance."

Dave chuckled. "Ya probably don't want to know,

Captain," he replied without turning his attention away from Sarah.

"Hmmm, I imagine you're right," Clint said, grinning. "I'm sure it's way too personal for my tender ears to hear."

Mike let go with a slight chuckle of his own before tapping Clint on the arm.

"I wouldn't wait up for 'im tonight, Clint," Mike recommended, followed by another light chuckle. "I have a feelin' that boy will not be comin' in until the rooster crows."

"Hadn't planned on it, Mike," Clint answered, with a slight grin. "No, sir—hadn't planned on it."

Dave didn't hear a word they said. He was too busy thinking about his and Sarah's future. There wasn't much doubt in his mind that he was going to marry that girl.

Sarah glanced over at Dave when she had finished taking the customer's order. Her heart was racing as she smiled at him.

Dave quickly winked at her and returned the smile. In a couple of hours he would be in her arms again, and enjoying her sweet, heavenly kisses. He could barely contain his emotions.

Chapter Eighteen

Thursday, October 15th.

Clint arose early and walked over to the Tonto Basin Stage Line's branch office. He knew the stagecoach would be traveling east today, and he wanted the driver to carry a message to Robert at the Double Creek Ranch way station, and to his wife, Connie, at the café. As he approached the stage office, he spotted his good friend, and seasoned stagecoach driver, Hank Burley.

"Howdy, Hank!"

"Well, my stars! What ya doin' in Payson this early in the mornin', Clint?"

"I'm, *finally*, on my way home."

"Glad to hear it. I missed yer ol' face at the way station this past week. Robert said ya was off chasin' outlaws again."

"Yeah, that's a fact. Been down to Four Peaks. I arrived back in Payson yesterday afternoon—along with Ranger Martin and Marshal Chandler."

"Robert didn't say where ya'd gone. What in thunder was brewin' at Four Peaks?"

"Well, uh, the governor summoned lawmen from all over the territory to bust up a large gang of outlaws hidin' out in that area. It turned into a bloody mess. But we gave back as good as we got."

"Any lawmen hurt?"

"We lost a total of seven men. Two were rangers. Captain O'Bryan was wounded."

"Sorry to hear that, Clint."

"Well, I reckon it could have been a lot worse."

"Were *you* hurt, my friend?"

"Not so much. I got my arm sliced up a bit—nothin' serious though."

Clint pointed at the location of his wound, but his long-sleeved shirt hid the bandage.

"Say, I heard 'bout the bank robbery here in town yesterday. That deputy and citizen git'n killed was a darn sad deal," Hank said.

"Those four killers were members of the Kantrell gang that was hidin' at Four Peaks. They shot their way through our blockade. It's a rotten shame they ended up here in Payson."

"I'm just glad ya are okay ... and Mike, too."

"One of 'em surrendered. We've got him locked up. He'll most likely hang for his misdeeds."

"As he darn well should," Hank said as he shook his head.

Clint sighed. "It seems like crime is ever on the rise these days. There's no longer any respect for life. God's laws have been cast aside—so it seems."

Hank grunted. "Yup. I hear that."

Clint, desiring to discuss something of a more pleasant nature, changed the subject.

"Hank, you'll be stop'n at Christopher Creek today for lunch, right?"

"Shore will—just like I always do."

"Can you do me a small favor?"

"Certainly, my friend. Just name it."

"Since you'll be leavin' town long before me—I need a message delivered to Robert at the way station and to Connie at the café."

"Shore, Clint. Have ya got it written down?"

"No need. Just tell 'em both that I'm fine ... and that I should be ridin' in late this afternoon."

"I shore will do that."

"Thanks," Clint said as he shook Hank's hand. "Have yourself a safe journey, Hank. I'll be seein' you again on Friday at Robert's way station."

"See ya on Friday, Clint!"

Clint went back to his shared hotel room and rousted Dave from his soft, comfortable bed.

"Up and at it, Dave. We're to meet Mike at the café in twenty minutes. You gotta hustle, my friend."

"Okay, Captain. I'll git ... (yawn) ... up. I don't want to miss breakfast."

"What *you* don't want to miss is *Sarah*. What time did you get in last night, anyway?"

"Gosh, Captain, I don't rightly know. I don't own a watch. Reckon it could have been ... (yawn) ... near midnight—maybe later."

"Should you be keepin' that gal up so late? What are her folks gonna think?"

"Now there's a sad story, Captain. Her father is dead, and her sickly mother is strugglin' to hold on to their

modest little house on the edge of town. Sarah is suppor-
tin' 'em both. She ain't got no siblings—or other family
that she knows of."

"Are ya drawn to this gal because you feel sorry for
her and hope to be her *knight in shining armor*?"

"Oh, no, sir. I fell for her long before I heard her story.
But I do think I could help her if I had a job in this town.
I'd be doin' it out of love for her."

"Maybe you *are* the solution to her problem. Just the
same—before you go jumpin' in with both feet—you need
to pray about it."

Twenty minutes later, Clint and Dave were on their
way to the café to meet with Mike.

At the café, Sarah and Dave could hardly keep their
eyes off of each other. Mike commented that he would
have to bring Dave along with him to the restaurant every day just so he could continue to get such wonderful
priority service. Everyone chuckled at his rather reasonable comment.

"Dave, I want to offer ya a job. I need a new deputy. I
talked with the city fathers last night ... and they said it
would be okay to hire ya."

"Oh, that would be grand, Mike. When can I start?"
Dave asked. "Aw rats! I just remembered—I can't do anything until January."

"Yeah, I know. I heard that the rangers had to hang
on until then in order to collect their severance pay. But
I've got a plan."

"What kind of plan?" Dave asked as he focused intently on Mike for the answer.

"I'm gonna wire Major Williamson in Flag' and ask 'im
to reassign ya to Payson for the rest of the year. Of course,

I'll have to wire Captain O'Bryan, too. I need his approval as well—'im bein' yer immediate supervisor and all."

"Yeah, that's certainly a good idea. But he's in Mesa City, and won't be back at his desk at Fort Verde until Monday mornin'. That's when I'm supposed to report back as well."

"Oh, that's right. I had completely forgotten."

"I'd hate to travel all the way to Fort Verde ... and then, have to turn around and come back here. Everything I own I got with me, so I don't need to fetch a thing."

"If Williamson gives *his* permission, then I'm shore ya can stay here until I can get in touch with Captain O'Bryan." Mike paused, then asked, "What do *you* think, Captain Wells?"

"Hey, if it's God's will ..."

"I pray it is His will," Dave breathed.

"I'll be git'n that wire sent out as soon as we finish our breakfast," Mike promised.

"Captain, when are ya ridin' out to yer ranch?" Dave asked as he shoveled another loaded fork of fried potatoes into his mouth.

"As soon as we finish our meal. But first, I've got to notify the hotel clerk that I'm leavin', and then collect my things."

"Dave, will you be stayin' another night at the hotel?" asked Mike.

"No, I'll be lookin' around for somethin' a little bit cheaper. Maybe I can sleep at the stable."

"Dave, ya can sleep *free* at my office. I've got an empty cell with a comfortable bed. It'll do ya for a few nights," Mike said. "Besides, I need an extra set of eyes watchin' that prisoner. Don't' forget—he's still got a friend roamin' loose 'bout the countryside."

"The price is certainly right. I'll take it!"

After breakfast, Mike returned to his office. Clint and Dave went to the hotel to check out. From there, Dave ventured over to the marshal's office to join ranks with Mike. Clint went to the livery stable to get Apache ready to travel.

Twenty minutes later, Clint walked Apache up to the hitching rail in front of the marshal's office. He wrapped the lead rein around the rail and walked inside the office. Mike was sitting at his desk with his feet resting on top of it. Dave was sitting across the room next to the woodstove.

Clint pulled up a chair and sat down near Mike.

"Hey, Clint, I was hopin' ya'd not leave without sayin' goodbye," Mike said.

"I wouldn't do that."

"I know," Mike replied. "Anyway, I got some news for ya. I was just sharin' it with Dave."

"*Good news*, I pray?"

"Yep. A message came in over the wire a few minutes ago. It's 'bout that one outlaw that got clean away from us down at Four Peaks."

"You talkin' about the one ol' boy that none of us bothered to go chasin' after?"

"That would be the one."

"What does your wire say?"

"It seems he made it to Globe. And, yesterday afternoon, he tried to rob the local bank."

"You don't say."

"But it didn't work out so well for 'im."

"What happened?" Clint asked, most anxious to know the outlaws fate.

"Well, there was an elderly lady in the bank who was packin' a small caliber pistol ... and she got the drop on 'im. Our would-be robber is now fillin' a jail cell at the county lockup."

"Good news, huh, Captain?" Dave said.

"I know a widow lady that lives in Globe. She runs an upscale boardin' house," Clint said. "Did the wire mention the brave lady's name?"

"Yep, it did. Her name is ... uh ... Esther Day."

"Hey, by golly, that's her! Hooray for Esther!" Clint exclaimed.

"How is it that ya know her?" Mike asked.

"She's a good friend of Connie's. They came out on the stagecoach together from Holbrook back in '92. And, my friends, she's one tough lady."

"Ha! It's a small world," Dave replied.

"I can't wait to tell Connie. She'll get a big kick out this story," Clint said with a chuckle.

"I have no doubt," Mike agreed.

"Who was the thief? Got a name?" Clint asked.

"Name's Dexter Hobbs. He's wanted in Colorado for horse stealin'. I got a wanted poster on 'im last winter," Mike replied.

"Is there a reward?" Clint inquired.

"Five hundred dollars!" Mike gleefully announced.

"Lady Esther will be shop'n 'til she drops," Clint joked.

"Good for her!" Dave chirped.

"And it's good to have another outlaw in jail. Maybe if we can get this big piece of real estate, called Arizona, cleaned up—well, just maybe we can finally be approved for statehood in the very near future," Mike commented.

"Now, *that* would certainly be a move in the right direction!" Clint agreed. "I know the governor is certainly workin' hard on that goal."

"I could buy into statehood, too," echoed Dave.

Clint scooted his chair back and stood up. "Gents, I've got to stir up some trail dust. It's been great servin' with you both," he announced as he extended his hand to Mike and then to Dave. "God bless the both of you."

"Thanks, Clint. Say 'hello' to the wife. Maybe I can sashay over that way for a visit one of these days," Mike said. "It's much more likely to happen now that I've got this here new deputy."

"You're always welcome, Mike. That invite goes out to you, too, Dave."

"Thanks, Captain. I'll definitely keep that in mind. I really would like to visit your place again … and git the high-dollar tour. Captain O'Bryan and Will Clowers said it was a real nice ranch. Lots of pretty meadows and such."

"Speakin' of Will, I oughta make a trip to Show Low soon and see how he's doin' as the new sheriff," Clint remarked.

"I think he would like that," Mike said.

"*¡Adios, mi amigos!*" Clint said as he departed the office.

Clint mounted his colt, Apache, and reined him toward the east. He couldn't wait to get home to his wife and daughter. He would be counting down the hours. Tonight he would be in his own bed. Next to him would be the woman he loved with all his heart.

* * * * *

232

The Tonto Basin Stage Line coach, with Hank Burley at the helm, stopped at the café in Christopher Creek around eleven-thirty. This was a normal stop for the stage so that the passengers could have a hot meal on their way to Show Low. Three passengers disembarked.

Connie greeted the passengers from the porch of the café, and held the screen door open for them.

"Connie!" Hank shouted as he walked toward her. "Got some wonderful news for ya."

"What's up, Hank?" she said as she wiped her hands on her apron.

"Talked to Clint this morning. He's—"

"You did!" Connie exclaimed. "Where is he?!"

"He's in Payson ... and doin' just fine. Says to tell ya that he'll be home this afternoon."

"Oh, my! Oh, that's great news!" Connie said as she leaned forward and planted a big kiss on Hank's un-shaven cheek.

"Wow! I'll have to talk ol' Clint into givin' me *more* messages in the future," he said as a big grin formed on his weather-beaten, wrinkled face.

Connie smiled. "Does Robert know?" she asked.

"Yup. I shore told 'im, ma'am," he reported.

Connie ran next door to the mercantile store and told her aunt the good news.

"I declare, we'll not get a lick of work out of you for the rest of the day," Helen Myers joked as she hugged her niece.

"I wouldn't argue that point with you," Connie said with a chuckle.

When Connie returned to the café, sixteen-year-old Maree Reavis came running up to her. "Did I hear you say that Uncle Clint was coming home today?"

"You heard correctly, my dear. Isn't it wonderful?"

"Yes, it is. I hope he comes to the café so I can see him too," Maree remarked.

"Oh, I'm sure he will, Maree. I don't picture Clint going home and pacing about while he waits for me to close the café and come home," Connie reasoned, hoping she was right.

"Yes, I'll bet you're right."

"Maree, do you think you could handle things here by yourself for about thirty minutes?"

"Certainly. What are you going to do?"

"I'm going to run over to Pamela Mayne's place and pick up Lena. She's been caring for Lena the past few days while your mother recovers from her injury." (Jenny Reavis-Rhodes had the misfortune of being kicked in the thigh by a horse. It didn't' break the bone, but she was badly bruised, and limping to get around.)

"She's at the Circle M Ranch, right?"

"Yes, that's right," Connie readily confirmed. "It's not too far from here."

"Oh, Clint would just love it if Lena were here, too. Do go and get her. I'll be fine here. We've only the three patrons. Don't worry about a thing."

"Are you certain?"

"Yes, now go!" Maree exclaimed.

Connie took off her apron and walked back to the mercantile store to inform her aunt of her plan to pick up Lena. Her aunt immediately approved, and whisked her out the door. "Go! We'll be fine."

"Yes, ma'am," Connie said, happily.

"And don't you get in such a hurry that you end up in an accident!" Aunt Helen cautioned as Connie put the buggy into motion.

As she maneuvered the buggy down the road, Connie suddenly began to think about what her husband's condition might be. She thought he might be injured ... and that he kept his injury from Hank. Or that he could possibly be worn to a frazzle and would need time alone to recuperate before being pounced on by family and friends.

No! Hank said he was fine. And he should know—he saw Clint and talked to him. Hank wouldn't hide the truth from me, she muttered aloud as she wholly dismissed her worries.

I hope he isn't too tired—because I'm going to love him tonight like never before, Connie muttered quietly to herself. *Yes, indeed! He's going to know that his woman missed him with all her heart and soul.*

* * * * *

It was around two o'clock when Mike received a reply to the message he had sent to Major Williamson.

Williamson sent his condolences to Mike concerning the death of his deputy. He also mentioned that he had received a wire from Captain O'Bryan concerning the deaths of Ranger Loomis and Ranger Green. The final part of Williamson's message was the approval of Dave Martin's request to remain in Payson. He said reassignment orders would soon follow by mail.

Dave Martin was overjoyed by the news. He ran immediately to the Yellow Sun Café to inform Sarah of the good news. To say she was thrilled would be an understatement.

The owner of the café, Betsy Lovemore, offered her congratulations. If there was one thing Betsy loved most, it was a happy employee.

"I hope this doesn't mean that you'll be leaving me?" Betsy asked. "You're the best waitress I've got."

"Oh, not at all," Sarah replied. "I like working here very much."

"That's a relief," Betsy sighed. "I hope you'll invite me to the wedding."

"Oh, of course! I wouldn't dream of you not being there," Sarah quickly declared.

"Good. Reckon I'll make the wedding cake when that day gets here," Betsy concluded as she walked back into the kitchen.

* * * * *

It was nearing four o'clock when Clint reined up in front of the café at Christopher Creek. He was so excited that his hands were shaking. Finally, he was back in his own neighborhood. The trip to Four Peaks had served up more excitement than he bargained for—but now it was time for peace and quiet and, most of all, family.

Clint walked up the short flight of wide steps to the café's porch. As he was about to reach for the door handle, a beautiful raven-haired woman snapped open the door and rushed into his arms. She plastered his entire face with kisses before aiming squarely for his lips. Clint could feel her body burning with passion as he held her in his arms. He was enjoying every single minute of her aggressive behavior.

Finally, he stepped back to look at her. Her breathing was heavy and her breasts heaved in rhythm with each breath. Her face radiated with happiness. The smile on her face and the look in her eyes spoke volumes. He had been away from this lovely woman for seven days, and at this very moment she was letting him know that she was overjoyed to have him back in her presence.

"Wow! I'm stoppin' at this café more often," he declared. "Do your *other* diners get this brand of welcome to your café?" he asked jokingly as a big grin spread across his face.

"No, only the *special* ones," she replied teasingly. "And it doesn't end with just hugs and kisses."

"Well, ma'am, I certainly like bein' *special*," he said as he squeezed her hand gently and winked.

Connie led her husband inside the café and sat him down at a table in the corner. She immediately motioned for Maree to come over and join them.

Maree gave her uncle a big hug and a kiss. Besides being a wonderful niece, she was also a very good waitress—with her sights on becoming a great chef. Connie was helping her achieve that goal by teaching her the fine art of country-style cooking.

"Are you hungry, Uncle Clint?"

"Yes, indeed, missy. What have you got cookin' in that ol' kitchen of yours that would excite my taste buds?"

"Pot roast. And it's really good. I made it all by myself," Maree responded with pride.

"Well, missy, bring it on!" Clint said as he patted her rosy cheek.

"I'll be back with your meal in a second, Uncle Clint," she said as she scurried off to the kitchen.

"Clint," Connie began, "excuse me just a minute while I go next door and tell Aunt Helen that you've arrived."

"Oh, please do. I just wish Lena were here."

Connie was gone for only a brief moment when Clint suddenly heard a lone voice calling out to him. He spun around in his chair and saw little Lena running to him.

"Daddy! Daddy!"

Clint jumped from his chair and scooped her up into his arms. He hugged her gently and began kissing her ruddy cheeks. She gladly returned kiss for kiss.

Connie returned with her aunt.

Mrs. Myers expressed sincere words of welcome and gave Clint a hearty hug. After a short chat, she returned to the store.

Connie wrapped her right arm around Clint as he continued to hold Lena. Clint leaned over and gave his wife a kiss on the cheek. She readily blushed.

"Ah, it's so good to be home with my family again!" Clint declared for all in the café to hear. "I have been truly blessed. Praise God!"

"Yes, praise God," echoed Connie as she kissed her husband again.

THE END

Epilogue

It's been a year since our story ended. So it's time to re-view the past year and see what has happened to some of our principal characters since then.

Clint Wells received some outstanding news last Christmas Eve. His wife, Connie, informed him that she was pregnant. This past July, she gave birth to a baby boy. They named him Cody Lynne Wells. Lena is thrilled about her new baby brother.

This past May, Clint finally brought an old idea that he had back in 1894 to fruition; he is now the proprietor of a *dude* ranch. Chip Bowman is his official foreman and head wrangler. Clint has since hired three more cowboys to help with the operation. A larger bunkhouse had to be built to accommodate all the Easterners that have flocked to his place for fun and adventure.

Recently, Clint and Connie traveled to Mesa City. As the stagecoach came into view of Four Peaks, Clint couldn't help but wonder how a place so scenic could have been the location of such a bloody battle for law and order in the Arizona Territory.

Following the disbandment of the Arizona Rangers in January, **Major Tom Williamson** left Flagstaff with his wife, Linda, and moved to Biloxi, Mississippi. He is cur-rently studying to be a minister.

Following the disbandment of the rangers, **Captain Jim O'Bryan** left Fort Verde and moved to Phoenix. Not long after arriving, he met, and soon thereafter, married a local girl. His wife, Sheila, is supporting his efforts to run for political office.

Dave Martin left the rangers and became the chief deputy for Marshal Mike Chandler in Payson. He married Sarah Benson shortly after taking the job. They share a house with her mother on the edge of town. Sarah still works at the Yellow Sun Café—and Dave is still her favorite customer.

Geoff Tingle left the rangers and moved to Dayton, Ohio, where he started a freight company. He is now a successful businessman. His company delivers dry goods from wholesalers to mercantile stores all over the Mid-West.

Sheriff Will Clowers, a former ranger, is still living and working in Show Low. Several months ago, he married a girl that had come to the West from Rockwood, Tennessee. He and his wife, Becky, have adopted a little boy.

Maree Reavis, now seventeen, is dating Chip Bowman. It looks pretty serious. Maree is still working at Connie's café located at Christopher Creek. She is now the head chef and loves her work. However, she still helps out with the waitress duties whenever the new girl gets behind on her tables.

Robert Lynne (Connie's brother) recently bought the rights to the Tonto Basin Stage Line when it was put on the market as part of an estate sale. Robert renamed it a few months ago. It's current name: Double Creek Transit Company. And, to meet demand, it's been expanded to two stagecoaches—an east *and* west coach—that operate daily, except on Sunday.

Chino Watson left the rangers and became a brakeman for the Santa Fe railroad. He now lives in the tiny community of Ash Fork, Arizona Territory. He still rides the horse once owned by his best friend, Dewey Loomis. Chino has never forgotten the day the outlaw, Russ Thorpe, killed his friend at Four Peaks.

A personal message from the author:

You have just finished reading the third book in the western novel series—*Clint Wells, Arizona Ranger.* I hope you enjoyed the story.

Sadly, for me at least, this is the last book in the series. I thank you, my readers, for your interest in my work. If you haven't read the first two books—please do so. I think you will enjoy reading them as much as I did writing them.

I pray that all your trails will be happy and adventurous.

¡Adios!

Coming in 2012:

Rider from the High Lonesome.

About the Author

CRAIG MAIN, a United States Air Force retiree and "baby boomer," is an inspiring new author of western novels. *Four Peaks: The Final Campaign* is his third novel, and the last in the Clint Wells, Arizona Ranger trilogy. It is the sequel to *Raiders of Salt River Canyon*, which was a sequel to *Shadow of the Mogollon Rim*.

Though relocating recently to his hometown of French Lick, Indiana, he lived in Arizona for most of his adult life—beginning in January 1965. Arizona still had a significant Wild West ambiance in the sixties, and numerous unspoiled places were always waiting to be discovered. Many ranchers still rode their horses into town on a regular basis. Western wear was the uniform of the day.

Craig spent a good deal of his free time camping, hiking, mountain biking, and hunting throughout central and northern Arizona, which includes the Four Peaks, Salt River Canyon and Mogollon Rim regions. He is very familiar with the locations mentioned in this exciting new novel, and has even driven his four-wheel drive vehicle to the top of Four Peaks. (The Brown Trailhead is located in the "saddle" between the peaks.) His character, Clint Wells, reflects his Western spirit. This is a novel that young adults and "baby boomers" alike can enjoy.